I miss you, too, sport,

Joe thought as he tucked his son's latest letter into his shirt pocket. One thing about Max's letters always remained consistent: Max never failed to ask when Joe was coming home.

He picked up Max's photograph. I miss you more every day I'm here, he thought. It's bad enough that you've had to grow up without a mother—now you have to do without a father, too. But I'll make it up to you, Max, when I finally get home. I swear I will, son.

There were times when the guilt was overwhelming. Those were the times Joe had to remind himself that he was here for something important, that in the long run, it would benefit Max and all the kids all over the world. Joe told himself the peacekeeping effort was a guarantee for the future of kids everywhere.

If only Joe had a guarantee that when Christina learned he had a son, she wouldn't write a "Dear John" letter....

Dear Reader,

What a fabulous lineup we have this month at Silhouette Romance. We've got so many treats in store for you that it's hard to know where to begin! Let's start with our WRITTEN IN THE STARS selection. Each month in 1992, we're proud to present a Silhouette Romance novel that focuses on the hero and his astrological sign. This month we're featuring the charming, handsome Libra man in Tracy Sinclair's *Anything But Marriage*.

Making his appearance this month is another one of our FABULOUS FATHERS. This delightful new series celebrates the hero as father, and the hero of Toni Collins's *Letters from Home* is a very special father, indeed.

To round out the month, we have warm, wonderful love stories from Pepper Adams, Geeta Kingsley, Vivian Leiber, and as an added treat, we have Silhouette Romance's first PREMIERE author, Patricia Thayer. PREMIERE is a Silhouette special event to showcase bright, new talent.

In the months to come, watch for Silhouette Romance novels by many more of your favorite authors, including Diana Palmer, Annette Broadrick and Marie Ferrarella.

The Silhouette Romance authors and editors love to hear from readers, and we'd especially love to hear from *you*.

Happy reading from all of us at Silhouette!

Valerie Susan Hayward
Senior Editor

LETTERS FROM HOME
Toni Collins

Published by Silhouette Books New York
America's Publisher of Contemporary Romance

If you purchased this book without a cover you should be aware that this book is stolen property. It was reported as "unsold and destroyed" to the publisher, and neither the author nor the publisher has received any payment for this "stripped book."

In loving memory of Babs
October 5, 1991

SILHOUETTE BOOKS
300 E. 42nd St., New York, N.Y. 10017

LETTERS FROM HOME

Copyright © 1992 by Moonstone/Solitaire, Inc.

All rights reserved. Except for use in any review, the reproduction or utilization of this work in whole or in part in any form by any electronic, mechanical or other means, now known or hereafter invented, including xerography, photocopying and recording, or in any information storage or retrieval system, is forbidden without the permission of the publisher, Silhouette Books, 300 E. 42nd St., New York, N.Y. 10017

ISBN: 0-373-08893-0

First Silhouette Books printing October 1992

All the characters in this book have no existence outside the imagination of the author and have no relation whatsoever to anyone bearing the same name or names. They are not even distantly inspired by any individual known or unknown to the author, and all incidents are pure invention.

®: Trademark used under license and registered in the United States Patent and Trademark Office and in other countries.

Printed in the U.S.A.

Books by Toni Collins

Silhouette Romance

Ms. Maxwell and Son #664
Letters from Home #893

Silhouette Desire

Immoral Support #686

TONI COLLINS

is a bestselling author of mainstream novels under her real name. She has worked in numerous occupations, all with one goal in mind: to one day realize her dream of being a full-time writer.

When Ms. Collins began writing for Silhouette Books, she felt a greater freedom with the category romance format, since she felt that she "could do things in these books that simply didn't fit" her mainstream books.

Ms. Collins has traveled extensively and now lives in St. Louis with her son.

Fatherhood...

Dear Dad,

You're the one in the army, but I'm the one who has to answer to the general! Grandma and I miss you, Dad. When are you coming home?

Love, Max

★

Dear Christina,

Nothing makes me remember how precious life is, quite as strongly as the birth of a baby. I'd love to have a whole houseful of kids. What about you? How do you feel about children?

Love, Joe

★

Joe wondered if Christina received his last letter. How she responded to that letter could have a major impact on his future—and his son's. Max was always going to be his primary consideration....

Chapter One

We might as well have been born on different planets, Christina thought as she read the letter again.

It had all started months ago—longer than that, actually—when she'd written several letters addressed simply to "Any Soldier" stationed in the Persian Gulf. She, like millions of other Americans, had been writing letters of support and encouragement to servicemen and women who were part of the U.S. military force there long before Operation Desert Shield became Operation Desert

Storm and the conflict turned into full-scale war.

But unlike millions of other Americans, Christina hadn't stopped writing when the war ended. To those who bothered to ask why she continued, she pointed out that military personnel were still there as part of the UN's peacekeeping plan. Those men and women had to be just as lonely now as they had been during the fighting—maybe even more so than before, since they didn't have the war to keep their minds off the loneliness that plagued most of them.

For Christina Holland, daughter of a senator who had been one of the strongest supporters of the military action against Iraq, the American presence in the Middle East was the stuff of dinner-table conversations. The more she listened to her father's nightly reports on the situation, the more convinced she was that her letters were needed now more than ever. During the war, she had several Gulf "pen pals," and she wrote them all regularly. Most of them were men, and most of their letters were filled with details about the war—and afterward, the rebuilding of Kuwait and other areas that had been heavily bombed. She enjoyed corresponding with them all, though she found it amusing that once the men found out what she looked like, they pulled out all the stops to impress her.

At twenty-nine, Christina—Chris, to her friends (except her father, who had never called her *anything* but Christina)—was a very attractive woman. Of medium height, she was slim but not boyishly so. Her long hair was thick and dark, almost a coffee brown, and her large, wide-set eyes were even darker. Her features were finely chiseled and her smile the best her father could buy. She was beautiful and she knew it, but she had never thought of her looks as an advantage or an asset. If anything, they had been a hindrance in her relationships with men. The men she'd known had never bothered to look past her face and body long enough to get to know the woman behind them.

Until now.

The man who had written the letter she held in her hand seemed much more down-to-earth than the men she was accustomed to. He didn't go out of his way to impress her. His letter was straightforward, honest and without pretense....

Dear Christina,
Your letter came as a complete surprise. I didn't think anyone was writing letters to "Any Soldier" anymore. Once the war was over, we seemed to have been forgotten.

My name is Joe Parrish. I'm a private in the army. I don't have any great war stories to tell you, since I didn't get here until long after the fighting was over. I'm part of what the fellows in Washington refer to as the "peacekeeping effort...."

Christina smiled to herself. The "peacekeeping effort"—her father's words exactly. She decided it probably would be best not to tell her father this Private Parrish had referred to Congress as "the fellows in Washington," though. She read on...

I come from Indiana, from a town so small it's never been on any map, so I'm sure you've never heard of it. My father's an autoworker. He should have retired years ago, but he can't afford to. Too many kids. There are seven of us, all grown now. Dad's still paying bills from our childhood expenses. Mom doesn't work, never has—though we would have been better off if she had. Dad always said she didn't work because it would have cost them more for a baby-sitter when we were all little than she could have earned at the kind of jobs she was qualified for. I'm the oldest—just turned twenty-nine. I have two brothers and four sisters. Try getting into the bathroom first thing in the morning, when you've got one bathroom and five women in the house...

Christina tried not to laugh. There were three women in the Holland household, counting the maid, and they had six bathrooms!

Still it's kind of nice sometimes. Like the holidays. It's great having the whole family together. Holidays are a major event. We have two kitchen tables, and we take the doors off the hinges and put them on top of the tables to make them long enough to accommodate everybody. When my grandparents were still living, it got kind of embarrassing, because we needed even more table space, so Grandpa would go looking for an extra door to take down, and for some reason he always took the bathroom door!

This time Chris couldn't help laughing. She was glad he wasn't here, because he might think she was laughing at him. She tried to imagine what it must have been like—compared to one of the formal dinners at the White House, and she'd attended more than a few of those events. She could imagine some of the stuffed shirts she knew eating dinner off someone's bathroom door!

This man has a delightful sense of humor, she thought as she read on....

I went to college—I started, anyway. I left during my third year and enlisted in the army, because it seemed like the best thing to do at the time. We needed the money. I figure one of these days I'll go back to school. If I ever figure out what it is I'd like to do with my life.

Hope you'll write again soon and tell me more about yourself.

Cheers, Joe Parrish

Christina folded the letter slowly and returned it to its envelope. His letter sounded like an awkward first date—saying anything and everything in an attempt to make conversation. This Joe Parrish had practically taken a full inventory of himself in this letter. To her surprise, Christina was touched. None of the other men she'd known had ever behaved this way, even in person. There was something about it that was refreshing.

Certainly different from the men she was accustomed to—rich, blue-blooded men born with enough cocky self-assurance for ten men and enough money to spend on the kind of dates that made a lot of women willing to overlook a lack of conversational skills.

That description, she thought wryly, especially applied to the man she'd been engaged to. Thank God she'd come to her senses before the wedding actually took place.

She looked down at the letter in her hand again. He'd closed with the word *cheers*. A nice safe closing. Friendly, but not too intimate. Not as formal as "yours truly" or "sincerely."

Yes, she thought, pressing the envelope to her lips, this Joe Parrish could definitely be a pleasant—and welcome—change of pace.

"You're still writing letters? Hasn't anyone told you the war is over?"

This was Christina's best friend, Daphne Harris. Daphne's father was a Supreme Court justice. The Hollands and the Harrises had been friends for as long as Christina could remember. She and Daphne had grown up together, attending the same private schools, and had even been roommates at Vassar. Daphne was attractive, with long copper-colored hair and a slim, boyish figure that came from long hours spent on the tennis courts and in the nearest available pool. She was shockingly outspoken and had a ribald wit. She was engaged to a White House aide who had some pretty lofty political ambitions of his own—and probably saw Daphne as an entrée to the right places and people since he had money, but few connections of his own.

"We haven't completely withdrawn from the Gulf, you know," Christina reminded her. "There are still men and women stationed there, and right now I'd be willing to bet it's a pretty boring place to be stuck in." She paused. "There are also a lot of civilians—American civilians—over there working on the cleanup and restoration."

"And you're doing your patriotic duty," Daphne concluded, her tone only mildly teasing.

Christina didn't find the comment particularly funny. "If you want to call it that, yes," she stated flatly.

"Oh, come on—I was only kidding!" Daphne insisted, surprised by the response she'd received. "But I *do* think you have too much time on your hands. What you need is a man in your life."

"I *had* a man in my life. More than one, in fact," Christina pointed out. "I'd be better off with a good dog."

"You'd change your mind, if you were to find the right man," Daphne insisted firmly.

"And I suppose you just happen to know where I can find Mr. Right?"

"As a matter of fact—" Daphne began.

Christina raised a hand to silence her. "What's the matter, Daph—don't you think I can find a man on my own?" Christina chided her gently.

"So far, you have a lousy batting average in that department," Daphne pointed out undiplomatically. "You're twenty-nine years old and you've been engaged but never yet made it to the altar."

"This isn't baseball, Daph. And you haven't said 'I do' yourself—yet."

"But I will—very soon now."

"After being engaged to the same man for the past ten years."

"Nine," Daphne corrected. "And it was simply the practical thing to do—waiting to get married, I mean. Charles needed time to concentrate on his career. Besides, we weren't really *waiting,* if you know what I mean."

Christina knew exactly what she meant. And she was only too familiar with that universal excuse in political circles for postponing marriage—besides, she'd always been more than a little suspicious of the real intentions of Daphne's longtime fiancé, Charles Wendell Hunnicut. But she said nothing. It wouldn't do any good. Daph wouldn't listen.

No... Daphne would end up like so many women they both knew, married to a man who would always put his career first— ahead of her, ahead of their marriage, ahead of their family. She would be an asset to him politically—and that, more often than not, would be the extent of her importance to him.

Besides, Daphne could fulfill her end of the deal.

She didn't have to work. She wanted to.

Christina was an executive with a leading public-relations firm in Washington—Cabot, Kendall and Associates. One day, she'd promised herself, it would be Cabot, Kendall, *Holland* and Associates. Her father might have opened the appropriate doors to get her the position, but Christina's own talent and dedication had enabled her to stay there. She was good at her job—a fact no one could dispute.

Alone in her office with its impressive view of the nation's capital, she found herself thinking about Private Joe Parrish again. She thought about him a lot lately, wondering what he was really like—what he looked like, what his interests were, what he wanted in a woman. There was a certain fascination she couldn't quite define. Perhaps it had more to do with the fact that she was carrying on a relationship of sorts with a man she had never met. But then, he wasn't the only man she was writing to.

He was just the only one who had really captured her interest.

At any rate, she was definitely going to write him again.

"Chris?"

Startled, her head jerked up. Her assistant, Melissa Tennant, stood in the doorway. "What is it, Mel?" she asked distractedly.

"I've got a doctor's appointment. I'm going to be out of the office for a couple of hours," Melissa explained. "What do you want me to do about your phone?"

"Just have the switchboard cover it," she told the woman.

"Okay."

Melissa left the room, closing the door as she did so. Christina tried to turn her attention back to the project she'd been working on, but found herself unable to concentrate. She was thinking about Daphne, about the conversation they'd had the day before. On at least a couple of points, she had to admit—if only to herself—that Daphne had been right. She was now twenty-nine years old and of all the romances she'd had since her sixteenth birthday, only one of them had been serious enough to progress as far as the engagement stage. Even then, she'd failed to make it to the altar. She was still single, still living with her parents.

Lately, she'd begun to wonder if she was missing out on something.

She told herself a lot of women stayed single these days by choice. She told herself that she wasn't lonely, that she was perfectly happy living with her parents. Theirs was a big house and she could have privacy when she felt the need for it. But the truth was that she was simply making the best of an impossible situation. She had resigned herself to this way of life because she was convinced she would never have any other. Certainly none of the men she knew would ever want to marry her, knowing she could never have children.

She'd known since she was sixteen. She had been riding in competition—back then she had Olympic gold in her eyes—and had taken a bad fall. She'd been seriously injured—internal bleeding, doctors said then—and they had agreed a hysterectomy was necessary to save her life.

At the time, it hadn't mattered. She'd been grateful just to be alive. But later...later, when she realized how few men wanted to marry a woman who couldn't provide them with heirs, when she realized how much she herself wanted children...then, it mattered a great deal.

But she didn't want to think about that now. Thinking about it didn't help. She wanted to think about happy things, things that made her smile.

She thought about it for a moment before picking up the pen, then she started to write....

Dear Joe,
Talk about surprises! Your letter was different from any of the others I've received....

Chapter Two

Too bad she's on the other side of the world, Joe Parrish thought as he read Christina's letter. This is a woman I'd definitely like to get to know better...

Dear Joe,
Talk about surprises! Your letter was different from any of the others I've received. As I mentioned before, I've been writing to a lot of servicemen—and women—since before the Gulf War began. Most of the letters I've received have dealt primarily with the war it-

self—the action, the casualties, the concerns of the men. Even the letters I've received since the fighting stopped have been full of information about the cleanup and the restoration. Not that I'm not interested in those things, mind you—but people interest me more.

My mother would love this girl, Joe thought, wishing he had a cold beer instead of the tepid water he was sipping at the moment. He pulled off his cap and raked one of his large-boned hands through his dark blond perspiration-soaked hair. Behind the dark glasses he wore, his eyes were blue—though he suspected the sand had left them more red than blue today.

He read on....

I'm from the country, too. I don't know how the country in Virginia compares to the country in Indiana (you're right, I've never been there!). All I know is that I could never be a full-time city dweller. I love horses, I love to ride. I love living here on the farm. I grew up here—did I tell you that? I've lived here all my life, couldn't imagine living anywhere else. Our nearest neighbors—I live with my parents—are a mile away, but I think everyone within a ten-mile radius knows my pickup truck.

She lives with her parents. She drives a pickup truck, Joe thought. Yeah, Mom would definitely love her!

I'm an only child. I always wondered what it would be like to have brothers and sisters, always wondered how it would have felt to grow up part of a large family. There have been times I've felt maybe I missed out on something pretty wonderful. I guess with my father having to travel so much, it was a miracle my parents managed to have *one* child...

Her father must be a traveling salesman or something, Joe concluded, wishing he could take a long, hot shower and wash the sand out of his hair and off his skin. It was funny how you didn't really appreciate the so-called "little things" until you had to do without them.

He reread Christina Holland's letter, then folded it carefully, returned it to its envelope, and tucked it into the pocket of his uniform. He tried to imagine what she might look like. Blond? Brunette? Redhead? Was she tall? Short? Skinny? Curvy? Did she look like Julia Roberts—or Cyndi Lauper? Was she young? She seemed young in the way she wrote, the things she said.

She still lived with her parents. That in itself was unique. How many adults lived with their parents these days?

Oh, God, he thought. Please don't let her be some skinny teenage girl with pimples and braces! Is it possible? Sure, it's possible! One of his buddies wrote to a girl for six months before she told him she was only twelve years old.

Talk about knocking the wind out of a guy's sails!

Yep... Mom would love this lady. Especially after Mindy.

Mindy was Mindy Purcell, the girl back home, the woman who'd been the mother of his son. When he thought about it, he had to admit that Max was the only good thing to come out of their relationship. He should have known better than to get involved with her in the first place. He'd known Mindy all his life, known what she was like. They'd practically grown up together. He knew she was spoiled and self-centered and much too concerned with the pursuit of her own pleasure to ever be able to really care about anyone else—even her own child. But Mindy Purcell, for all of her flaws, had been the prettiest and most popular girl in town.

When they became an "item," Joe was considered a lucky guy—and for a while, he believed it himself. Until Mindy started showing her true colors. When she found herself pregnant, he saw the real Mindy for the first time. She'd been furious, insisting upon an immediate abortion. She didn't want a child. She didn't *ever* want a child. Children didn't fit into her plans. And she certainly couldn't see herself having to deal with dirty diapers, runny noses and sticky fingers.

She didn't want the baby—but to his surprise, Joe found that he did. It was all he could do to convince her to go through with the pregnancy—she was afraid it would ruin her figure—but she was only too happy to hand over the baby when he was born, and allow Joe to legally adopt him. She didn't see Max while she was in the hospital, and had made no attempt to see him in the ten years since. Joe hated what it did to Max, knowing his own mother didn't want him, but Joe told himself they were better off without her. Without her, and most of the other women he'd known—some of whom didn't give up easily, even though they weren't crazy about a package deal.

Women who seemed to be wild about him—but never quite accepted his son.

"Another letter from Mom?" Joe's buddy and bunkmate, Dave Jenkins, had come in and noticed the envelope lying on Joe's bunk.

"Nope." Joe removed his T-shirt, pulling it over his head. He shook the sand from it and tossed it aside, then unzipped his pants.

"Who, then?" Dave pressed him.

"Some woman in the States."

"Some woman? You don't know her?"

Joe shook his head. "It was one of those 'Any Soldier' letters," he offered in explanation.

Dave grinned. "Are people stateside still writing those?"

"She is, apparently."

Dave looked genuinely surprised. "I thought once the war was over, the folks in the States would forget some of us are still here."

"So did I. I guess we were wrong," Joe said with a shrug.

"I guess." There was a brief pause. "What's she like?"

"I don't know that much about her—yet," Joe admitted.

"Well, if she's got time on her hands, she must be a real dog—or as old as dirt. Young, good-looking women have better things to do than write letters to guys they don't know."

"Or she could be a kid," Joe remembered dismally, still wondering if Christina Holland could be someone's teenage daughter.

"Yeah—that was a good one, wasn't it?" Dave chuckled, realizing immediately what Joe was referring to.

"For some of us, I suppose," Joe said absently. Then he asked, "What'd you get? I heard your name called."

Dave frowned. "A letter from Josie." Josie was Dave's wife. They'd been married seven years now.

"How is she?" Joe asked, trying to be polite.

"Restless."

Joe knew better than to ask what his friend had meant by that. He knew what Dave meant without asking.

Josie, it seemed, was tired of being alone, tired of not having her husband around. That, more often than not, meant trouble.

Joe was glad *he* didn't have a wife waiting for him back home.

Sergeant Lewis was without a doubt the ugliest human being Joe had ever seen. His mother would have reprimanded him for the thought and reminded him that all of God's creations were beautiful, but Joe had a hard time believing that God could have created

Sergeant Lewis. The man had a face like a bulldog's.

On second thought, Joe decided the man was uglier than a bulldog. There really wasn't anything on earth ugly enough to compare him with. The worst part, though, was that his personality wasn't any better than his looks. If Joe had believed in reincarnation, he would have been certain Sergeant Lewis was the reincarnation of Attila the Hun.

But today, Joe's mind was not on Sergeant Lewis or how miserable the man had made his stay in the Gulf. Nor was it on the heat or the growling sounds coming from deep within the pit of his stomach. He was surprised to find himself thinking about the letter he'd just received, about the woman who'd written it.

He'd never given it much thought before it actually happened, but the idea of corresponding with a woman he'd never met, never seen in the flesh, was intensely appealing. It was sexy in a crazy kind of way. He could fantasize about her and she could look different each time he did. He could pass her on the street and would not know who she was.

What an intriguing thought!

The letters from Max always made Joe's day. They were often funny, always full of information he could have done without and lacking details of the things he wanted to know, and always very typically Max. The boy was a fine writer and had a vivid imagination, even at such an early age. The boy's going to be a writer, Joe thought proudly as he read the latest arrival....

> Hi, Dad!
> You're in the army and I'm the one who has to answer to the general. This isn't fair. Grandma is one tough cookie, doesn't let me get away with anything. Aren't grandmas supposed to *spoil* their grandchildren?
> I've been grounded the rest of the week for something dumb...

Something "dumb," Joe thought with mild amusement. Max didn't say what the "something dumb" was, but his vague description told Joe it must have been something major. Max was good at skirting issues. Joe wasn't worried—his mother had had years of experience in dealing with high-spirited boys.

Rowdy boys. Boys like him and his brothers.

No, he didn't doubt for a minute that his mother could handle anything Max dished out. But Joe missed having those moments with Max himself—even those when a little discipline was called for. And as much as Max adored his grandmother—in spite of recent complaints—Joe knew the boy needed a full-time father. And mother. And Joe needed a wife. Not a girlfriend. A wife.

His mother wouldn't have it any other way. All his mother ever wanted was for her children to be settled down and as happy as she had always been. And she was absolutely certain they couldn't be happy if they weren't married. In her eyes it simply wasn't possible.

No, they had to be married, preferably with children—and lots of them. Her grandchildren. Joe smiled at the thought. She'd been so adept at playing the matchmaker for her other children. His two brothers, Dean and Mike, had married women they'd grown up with. Dean's wife, Cindy, had just given birth to twins, Dean Jr. and Danny. Mike's bride, Linda, was pregnant—and the ink was barely dry on the marriage license (a fact his mother did not like to be reminded of). Joe's oldest sister, Sharon, had married the foreman at the auto plant where their father worked, and they had three kids. Anna was engaged to a man she'd known since the cradle. Eileen was married and expecting—Doc thought it could be triplets, she was already so big. And Donna Jean (the baby of the family), was seeing the same boy she'd been seeing since junior high.

He was the oldest—and the only real holdout. It wasn't that he didn't want to settle down. He did. Trouble was, while he'd met lots of attractive women, and had even been seriously involved with a few of them, he knew he had to be careful. He had Max to think about. He had to be sure the woman he married would not only be a good wife for him, but a good mother for his son.

Since it wasn't a decision he could—or wanted to—make tonight, he turned his attention to things he did need to do now. He picked up the pen and started to write....

Dear Christina,
Your latest letter came today....

Chapter Three

Christina brought the Maserati to a stop at the front gates and got out to check the mailbox. They must have been saving this down at the post office for the past two weeks, she thought as she flipped through the large stack of envelopes en route back to her car.

One of those envelopes caught her eye. It was an airmail envelope, with a military return address. Joe Parrish. Sliding behind the wheel of the Maserati, she put that one on the top of the stack in the passenger seat and stared at it for a moment. She considered opening it now, then changed her mind.

This is silly, she told herself. She hadn't done that sort of thing since she was a giggly schoolgirl eagerly awaiting responses to fan letters she'd written professing her undying love and loyalty to favorite rock stars. As she recalled, it had been a different star every few weeks back then. Fickle girl, she thought with mild amusement. You've always been fickle, haven't you?

The thought reminded her of Daphne's words: You just haven't met the right man.

Maybe I never will, Daph, she thought now.

She started the Maserati's powerful engine and headed up the long, tree-lined drive to the main house, a Georgian-style mansion that had been in the family for generations. Parking the car where she always did—it was almost a reflex action now—she grabbed the mail and her briefcase and went inside, calling out to her mother as she opened the front door.

"She's not here, Christina," responded the Hollands' maid, Marnie, who had been with the family since Christina was a little girl.

Christina put all of the mail that wasn't addressed to her on the table in the entrance hall. "She didn't go with my father, did she?" Christina asked Marnie. Win Holland had flown to London that day with two other senators to meet with the prime minister.

"Oh, no," Marnie said quickly. "She is at some sort of luncheon for the Arts and Education committee, I believe."

Christina nodded, smiling. She wasn't surprised. Music had been her mother's life since she was five years old. She was fiercely passionate about anything and everything concerning the arts. "I'll be up in my room," Christina told Marnie. "Will you let me know when my mother gets home?"

"Sure, Christina."

Christina took the steep winding staircase at a brisk clip. She went straight to her room—which was more a suite than a regular bedroom—and closed the door, an indication to Marnie and anyone else who might drop in that she didn't wish to be disturbed. Kicking off her shoes, she settled down on the bed and opened the letter from Joe Parrish....

Dear Christina,
Your letter came today. It made up for all of the things that have gone wrong this past week—and there's been a lot going wrong, believe me. You keep writing, and mail call will surely become the highlight of my miserable existence here.

I wrote to my mother today, too. Couldn't wait to tell her about you and your letters—not that I know all that much about you (but I sure would like to). I know she'll be thrilled we're corresponding. You can be glad neither of you is here with me, though—she'd be playing matchmaker. She'd prefer that we'd met in the flesh, if you'll pardon the expression, but at this point she wouldn't care how I met a woman, as long as I meet her. She never figured I'd meet anyone here, this way (if I sound a little forward, forgive me—that's just the way Mom is).

Socializing on any level isn't easy here. I've seen lots of women around, but we're not allowed to talk to any of them. Their heads and bodies are always covered—and most of the time they wear veils, too. You can't tell what they look like.

Drinking isn't allowed here, either. It doesn't bother me much, since I'm not a big drinker (I do like a beer every now and then), but most of the guys are pretty mad about it. I think not being able to drink bugs them more than not being able to date! If the Iraqis pulled anything now, they'd be facing off with one mean bunch of Americans! The days here seem endless sometimes. The nights are almost as bad. When I can't sleep, I think about the good times back home, before the war. I think about you now, too, Christina. I try to imagine what you look like, what your voice sounds like, what your perfume smells like...

Christina smiled to herself. In spite of the deceptively casual tone of the letter, he'd let her know that he thought of her as something more than a pen pal. Or was she reading too much between those lines?

He'd told his mother about her.

She had the feeling he had a less-than-accurate mental picture of her. He obviously saw her as the fabled girl-next-door type—and she was anything but. At least in respect to where Joe Parrish came from. Of course, that was her own fault. She'd done nothing to set him straight. If he wanted to see her that way, she was perfectly willing to let him.

If he knew the *real* Christina Holland, he might be disappointed. He might even stop writing. He might think they had too little in common. Most men didn't like the idea of a woman who had more money than they did, which was obviously the case here. She could tell him now and might never hear from him again.

She didn't want *that*.

"He asked for a photo. He wants to know what I look like," Christina told Daphne as they lounged by the Hollands' pool a few days later.

Daphne shrugged. "So what's the problem?" she wanted to know. "You're not exactly a bowwow, and you must have a few hundred good photos lying around. If you don't, there are a few hundred newspapers you could call for the file photo."

"That's exactly what I *don't* want," Christina told her. "He doesn't know who—or maybe I should say *what*—I am. I don't want to send him anything that might give it away."

Daphne laughed aloud at the thought. "He doesn't know who you are? He must've been in the desert a looooong time!" she immediately concluded.

"I'm serious, Daph," Christina said irritably.

"So am I," Daphne insisted with an impatient shake of her coppery curls. "Photos of you aren't exactly hard to find, and you're not an unknown by any stretch of the imagination."

"He hasn't made the connection between the Christina Holland who's been writing him and Senator Winthrop Holland. His father's an autoworker," Christina went on, sipping her lemonade. "I get the impression they're a real down-to-earth kind of family."

"Unless he's doing the same number on you that you've been doing on him," Daphne suggested.

"I'm not 'doing a number' on him!" Christina insisted indignantly.

"What would you call it?"

"Drop it, Daph." There was a warning note in Christina's voice. "He's for real. I'm sure of it. He's too open about his roots, his life before the war—"

"Maybe he does know who you are and just isn't saying so."

"No." Christina shook her head emphatically.

"So where does that leave you?" Daphne asked. "What do the two of you have in common?"

"Almost nothing," Christina admitted.

"And you're writing to him on a regular basis?"

"Weekly."

"Interesting," Daphne sighed. "This could prove verrrry interesting."

* * *

"Not going out this evening, dear?" Christina's mother asked.

At fifty-nine, Althea Morris Holland was still a trim, attractive woman—and a stylish one, with frequent appearances in *W* and *Women's Wear Daily* to her credit. Her career as a concert pianist kept her fulfilled and had helped her cope with her husband's long and frequent absences for many years, though her own public appearances were few and far between these days.

Christina gave her an affectionate peck on the cheek. "Not tonight," she answered her mother's question. "It's been a long day. I barely have enough energy for a long, hot bath and a couple of hours of TV."

"I'll have Marnie bring up a tray for you, then," Althea insisted gently.

Christina nodded. "Thanks, Mom. You're a godsend."

But Christina hadn't realized just how tired she really was until she fell asleep in the bathtub. She not only fell asleep, she dreamed. It was a surprising and in some ways puzzling dream...in which she had the most romantic interlude possible with a man whose face was a blur.

He was tall, he was dark, he was handsome. He had a wonderful smile and a deep, sexy voice. And the most incredible eyes she'd ever seen—but when she woke up, she couldn't remember what color they were. Nor could she recall his features precisely. She knew only that he was the most attractive, charming man she had ever met—and that, at least for part of the dream, he wore a military uniform.

Joe Parrish?

Christina thought about it as she dried off and slathered a fragrant body lotion over every inch of her flesh. Did she have more than a passing curiosity about her newest pen pal? That was silly. She didn't know him. They'd never met.

Still...

She cleansed her face, now devoid of any traces of makeup, then applied a moisturizer that smelled like almonds. Removing the towel wrapped around her head like a turban, she combed her damp hair. Then slipped on a nightgown and robe and settled down in front of the TV in her bedroom suite just as Marnie came in with her tray.

She was still thinking about the dream as she nibbled distractedly at her food. Yes... she was *very* curious about Joe Parrish. She'd been more than casually interested ever since his first letter arrived. More so than she'd been about any of her other correspondents. More so than she'd been about most of the men she knew personally... though she wasn't quite sure why.

But to the point of romantic fantasy? Now that *was* silly!

So why was she doing it?

She finished her dinner, then seated herself at the small writing desk in her sitting room. She took a few sheets of stationery— the ivory embossed linen her mother had bought for her—and an envelope from the drawer. After giving it a few moments' thought, she applied pen to paper and started to write...

Dear Joe,
I look forward to getting your letters....

Chapter Four

"Goon alert," Dave Jenkins announced, as he entered their tent. "Sergeant Lewis at three o'clock."

Joe looked up from the letter he'd been writing. "Just what I don't need right now," he said with an exaggerated groan. Signing off quickly, he reached for an envelope.

Dave grinned, realizing what Joe had been doing. "Another letter to your girlfriend?" he wanted to know.

Joe folded the letter, put it in the envelope and carefully licked the seal. "She's not exactly my girlfriend, Dave," he pointed out. "I mean, we've never even *met*."

"Stranger things have happened."

"Yeah, right." Joe shook his head, mildly amused, as he scribbled Christina's address on the outside of the envelope.

"Sure—look at all of the couples who met by mail during the war and got married when those boys went home," Dave reminded him.

"I'm not the type to propose marriage to someone I've never met," Joe assured him as he got to his feet.

"Never say never, my friend."

Their conversation was interrupted at that point by the loud roar of Sergeant Lewis's voice outside their tent. "Our master calls," Joe declared, keeping his voice down so the sergeant wouldn't hear him.

Dave let out a groan. "Sometimes I think a court-martial would be easier," he confided, as they prepared to exit.

Joe nodded in agreement. "I'd certainly rather stare down the barrel of an M-16 than look at Lunatic Lewis's ugly mug."

Joe looked back at the letter lying on his cot as they headed out, and only then did he realize that he still had not told Christina about Max.

Why haven't I told her? he asked himself.
He was proud of his son. Max was normally his favorite topic of conversation. When Max was a baby, Joe showed his baby pictures so often around town that his father had joked that people threw bricks when they saw him coming. Sure, he'd gotten a little gun-shy after having experienced so much rejection—toward him and his son—from the women in his life, but why was he holding back with Christina? It wasn't as if they had a relationship—at least not that kind of relationship.

He took the photo of Max from his wallet—the one he was never without—and stared at it for a long time. It was still beyond his comprehension that Max's mother could have turned her back on him so easily, that she could have not wanted him. How could she not want her own child? He was a wonderful kid, bright and happy and full of energy. Any woman in her right mind would be proud to claim him as her own.

In her right mind, Joe thought. That's always been in doubt where Mindy's concerned.

But it was apparently the case where a lot of other women were concerned, too. Or maybe those other women just weren't crazy about the idea of raising another woman's child. Either way, it made no sense to Joe.

No sense at all.

But then, there was little about the opposite sex that did make sense to him. The Feminine Mystique, indeed! Everything feminine was a mystique, as far as he was concerned.

Maybe, he thought, I really do belong here in the middle of the desert with a hundred guys who all look like John Wayne.

Christina's latest letter revealed yet another side of her personality—one that came as a pleasant surprise to Joe.

Dear Joe,
I look forward to getting your letters. They make me smile even when I don't feel much like smiling.

You asked for a photo. I was reluctant to send one at first—I'm not terribly photogenic—but here goes. Hope you're not *too* disappointed.

He laughed aloud when he took the photo from the envelope. It was the Bride of Frankenstein—one of those photos that came in the photo section of a new wallet.

So... the lady has a sense of humor, he thought, amused. My kind of woman. Definitely my kind of woman.

He read on....

Well, now that you've seen *that,* anything else is bound to be an improvement—right?

I'll send the real photo in my next letter. I promise.

He looked at the photo again, still chuckling. Yep... the lady has a real nice sense of humor, he thought, quite pleased by the discovery.

He was tempted to write and tell her he used to date the Bride of Frankenstein before her shotgun marriage, but as his mother

would say, it wouldn't be proper for a gentleman to kiss-and-tell.
Then she got serious.

I hope you don't mind my asking, but don't you have someone special waiting for you back home?

That shook him. He didn't think he'd been that transparent. But as he read further, he realized she hadn't been talking about his son.

A fiancée? A wife? Someone you've been seeing?

Nobody worth mentioning, Joe thought dismally.

You've written about your family and your hometown and your life there, but you've never mentioned a special woman.
Is there no special woman in your life?

Not at the moment, Joe thought, and not for a very long time now. Unfortunately.

I suppose I'm a fine one to talk. I have an absolutely dreadful track record in the romance department

Maybe she *does* look like the Bride of Frankenstein, Joe speculated idly.
That's a mean thought.

It may be that I'm just picking the wrong men, I don't know. I was engaged once, a long time ago. Actually, it was more like a business merger than an engagement, now that I think about it. Each of us had certain clearly specified obligations to the merger, none of them having to do with "love, honor and obey."
   I wasn't able to keep up my end of the deal, so it fell through.

She makes it all sound so cold and impersonal, Joe thought. What kind of man was she engaged to, anyway?

And if he really was as she described him, what could she possibly have seen in him?

If I'd known what he was really like from the start, I wouldn't have even gone out with him, let alone accepted his marriage proposal. But I didn't know. He seemed like such a wonderful man, the kind of man any woman would be lucky to marry.

How little I knew about him then!

I know the feeling, Joe thought. If I'd known what Mindy was actually all about, I would have avoided her like the plague.

But then, he conceded, I wouldn't have Max now.

I must sound desperate to you.

Not desperate, honey—just desperately unhappy. Joe felt a strong empathy for this woman who was so clearly disillusioned by the opposite sex.

He understood, because he'd been there himself.

It's not that, not exactly. I suppose it's just that the women's movement moved without me. I have a career, yes, and I do love my work—but a part of me, a big part, wants to be just like my mother. She's had a successful career *and* a good marriage, and her life has always been happy and full.

I want that, too.

You couldn't get odds on it in Vegas, sweetheart. The pessimism that surfaced within Joe since he'd been here in the Gulf made him uneasy.

It also made him doubt that anyone could truly "have it all."

Least of all me, he thought.

I'm sorry, Joe. Here I am, dumping on you when you must have a great deal on your mind already. I suppose I should close for now, but I'll write again soon.

Ah, Christina, he thought as he folded that letter and put it back in its envelope. If only you knew how much we do have in common!

The Bride of Frankenstein photo slipped through his fingers and fell to the cot. He picked it up and looked at it again, chuckling to himself. All this and a sense of humor, too, he thought.

He put the photo in his wallet. He'd use this one to have some fun with Dave later. Right now, he had move important things to attend to. He opened the letter from Max.

Hi, Dad!
We got our report cards today. I got two As, three Bs and two Cs. I got a C in science because Mr. McClelland hates me—but then, he hates everybody. We call him the Troll Who Lives in 422.

No, we don't get sex education this year. Sex doesn't exist at my school.

I can't wait for summer. I hate school.

Did Grandma tell you about Henry? I found him in the woods. He had a broken leg, and we took him to the vet and had it fixed. She's not too crazy about the idea of having a raccoon in the house, but I think I can talk her into letting him stay, at least until his leg heals...

Joe chuckled softly. A raccoon! This was one argument he was fairly certain Max was not going to win. His mother had already had one rather unpleasant experience with a raccoon when Joe himself was a boy. He'd brought home a baby raccoon who had been a wonderful pet—at first. Then he grew up—at which point he developed all of the destructive force of a hurricane. Needless to say, the raccoon's eviction from the Parrish home had been swift.

Joe read on.

> I've been trying to come up with an idea for a science project for school. I thought about doing the solar system. I could do it with plastic balls and doll pins—you know, the sun in the center and the planets revolving around it. The only thing I can't figure out is how to make it all move.
>
> Maybe I should just do something with leaves or bugs or something...

Joe shook his head, amused. That was his Max. His philosophy was, and always had been, When in doubt, bail out.

Sometimes, Joe wondered if that wasn't the safest attitude to have.

One thing about Max's letters remained consistent: he never failed to ask when Joe was coming home.

I miss you, too, sport, Joe thought every time he looked at Max's photo, which was often. *I miss you more every day I'm stuck here. It's bad enough that you've had to grow up without a mother—now you have to do without a father, too. It's not fair, but unfortunately there's nothing I can do about it.*

But I'll make it up to you when I finally get home. I swear I will.

There were times the guilt was overwhelming. Those were the times he had to keep reminding himself that what he was doing here was important, that in the long run it would benefit Max and all kids all over the world. He told himself the peacekeeping effort, no matter when or where it was taking place, was a guarantee for the future of kids everywhere.

"Sounds a little melodramatic to me," Dave had kidded him when he brought it up once in conversation. "I can almost hear 'Yankee Doodle' playing in the distance when you talk, pal."

"You don't think what we're doing here is important?" Joe asked, genuinely surprised by his friend's comment.

Dave shrugged. "I lost my idealism a long time ago, Eagle Scout," he said simply.

This bothered Joe. He knew a lot of the men—especially those who'd been here a long time—had become somewhat cynical. But he didn't expect it from Dave. Dave hadn't been here all that long. He hadn't seen any of the fighting. They'd both come long after the war was over.

Still... there *were* times Joe had to admit that he felt waves of cynicism himself from time to time. In addition to waves of unbearable homesickness.

"How's Josie?" Joe asked casually after Dave had finished reading his wife's latest missive.

"Having the time of her life," Dave said gravely. "She wants a divorce."

Joe's head jerked up. "What?"

Dave frowned. "Seems she's met someone—some jerk she works with. They used to have lunch together—first in the office, then outside the office. Then, after I ended up here and Josie started getting so restless, he stepped in, good pal that he's always been, and started taking her out to dinner—and I don't even want to venture a guess as to what else."

"You think she's been having an affair," Joe concluded, uncomfortable with this conversation.

"I'm not naive," Dave snorted angrily. He paused, raking a hand through his damp blond hair in a gesture of frustration. When he spoke again, his voice was considerably lower. "It's pretty obvious, isn't it?' he asked.

Joe wasn't quite sure what to say, what Dave *wanted* him to say. "So what are you going to do?" he asked finally.

"What *can* I do?" Dave's tone was grim. "I'm four thousand miles from home—and Uncle Sam isn't about to send me home to save my marriage. They'd have to send half the guys here back, if that were their policy. Too common a problem in the military to allow it to interfere with our *duty,* unfortunately. No... about all I can do from here is find myself a good lawyer stateside to stand in for me in divorce court.''

As Dave stalked out of the tent, Joe turned back to the book he'd been reading. After a while he gave up, unable to concentrate. He found himself dwelling on Dave and his problems. Dave had been telling the truth. This kind of marital breakup—or perhaps break*down* was the more appropriate word—was indeed common among the enlisted men. Too common. Joe had seen enough to have doubts.

This was one of those times he was glad it was a problem he didn't have to worry about.

Christina's photograph—the real photo—came two days later, and for Joe it was a most pleasant surprise. She definitely was not a twelve-year-old with pigtails and braces. She was beautiful. He had the distinct feeling he'd seen her before, but it was a feeling he quickly dismissed. They could not possibly have met before. Hers was the kind of face one wasn't likely to ever forget.

Dear Joe,
Here's the photo I promised—on the level this time. I hope you're not too disappointed.

Disappointed? Joe laughed aloud at the thought. He was anything but disappointed!

I found a number of photos lying around the house, but only a few good ones.

Yeah, right, Joe thought, chuckling to himself. This is a woman who probably couldn't take a bad photo if she tried.

I realize I'm taking a chance here, that once you've seen the photo you may never want to hear from me again....

"Not a chance!" Joe laughed loudly, forgetting that anyone else was within earshot. The lady knew how to flirt. She *definitely* knew how to flirt. He continued to read.

Not that it would be the first time.

"Yeah, right," Joe chuckled, shaking his head.

I lead a very solitary life, unfortunately.

I'll bet, he thought, amused. She was probably a homecoming queen. She probably dated the captain of the football team. Maybe she was even class president.

As a girl, I was the proverbial ugly duckling.

Ugly duckling? He smiled as he looked at her photograph again. Well, honey, if you *were,* you've turned into one heck of a swan!

I was shy, extremely self-conscious. My parents couldn't understand it. Neither of them were the least bit shy or self-conscious. I think they must have wondered from time to time if they had been given the wrong baby at the hospital.

When I first started school, things got even worse. I felt like a leper. I was so shy I couldn't talk to any of the other children, and they didn't go out of their way to talk to me, so I usually ended up alone. I had no friends, and I was miserable.

His heart went out to her. It was hard to imagine the beautiful woman in the photo she'd sent him as an awkward, introverted child who had no friends and spent so much time alone.

But having been through all that, she would be able to understand better than anyone else could how painful Max's life had been as a result of Mindy's detachment.

I didn't come out of it until I was almost ten and started riding in competition. That gave me confidence in myself, helped me come out of my shell.

Sort of like Max and his zoo, Joe thought fondly. Christina could be great for Max. She could give him the love and understanding he so desperately needed.

If she were willing.

Enough of this. I don't want to depress you.

Her mood seemed to change abruptly. From that point on, she was upbeat, cheerful and chatty making no further references to that time in her life, other than comments about her parents and the happy times they had all shared.

Joe found himself again wondering about her father. He wasn't sure what the man did for a living, or how much money he made at it, but he had the definite feeling that Christina's father adored her... and spoiled her. Fortunately, it hadn't made her a brat!

You haven't yet sent me a photo of yourself. Don't you think it's only fair to reciprocate? I've tried to imagine, time and time again, what you must look like, but each time I read one of your letters, you have a different face in my mind. One time, you're tall and dark with brown eyes, the next you're blond and blue-eyed. You might be a

redhead with freckles and green eyes, for all I know. Do you have a beard? A mustache? Do you wear glasses?
I'm curious....

Joe smiled, considering how he might "get even" with her for the Bride of Frankenstein photo. Finally, after much thought, he came up with an idea. He sat down, pen and paper in hand, and started to write....

Dear Christina,
Your photo—the second one—came as quite a relief, especially after the first one. I've never liked women with big hair....

Chapter Five

They looked like the perfect family.

Christina didn't know who they were or where they were from, but she was mesmerized as she watched them from the small sidewalk café where she and her mother had had lunch. The man was tall and blond, wearing slacks and a sport shirt. The woman was a petite redhead in a flowered sundress. But it was the child who caught Christina's eye—a boy, no more than three years old, blond like his father and clearly a handful for his mother. The woman didn't appear to be at all distressed, though, talking and laughing with her husband as she struggled to restrain the squirming child.

I wouldn't complain, either, if I were in your place, Christina thought enviously.

Her mother's words cut through her thoughts. "Do I even have to guess what you're thinking, dear?" Althea Holland asked with mild concern.

Christina shook her head, not trusting her own voice.

Althea reached across the table and covered her daughter's hand with her own. "I do understand, dear. I know what you must be feeling," she said quietly. "But times *have* changed, you know. Even in our circles, women are choosing careers more and more often over marriage and children. Isn't that what the ERA was all about?"

"It was about *choice,* Mother," Christina said with a heavy sigh. "If the option were open to me, I would *choose* to have a family."

"You could always adopt," her mother suggested. "God knows there are a good many children—too many, actually—out there who need parents more than you need a child."

Christina shook her head. "It would be fine with me," she said, "but you know all of the men I've been involved with. Can you imagine any of them being willing to even consider a child who didn't have their own blue blood flowing through his or her veins?"

"Well—" Althea began.

"They wouldn't even be willing to think about such a thing. They have a real problem with the idea of 'contaminating' their families' bloodlines," Christina reminded her.

"Maybe you've just been involved with the wrong men," Althea said then, taking a forkful of her shrimp salad.

Christina looked at her, not sure she'd heard correctly. "What?"

"Perhaps you should look outside our so-called social circle," Althea went on to explain.

Christina laughed. "Daddy would have your head for even joking about such a thing!"

Althea's eyes met hers, and her expression was quite serious. "I'm not joking, Christina—and for the record, your father wants your happiness above all else."

Christina shook her head as she dabbed at the corners of her mouth with her napkin. "I could imagine his response if I were to bring home a blue-collar worker," she said, pushing her chicken salad around on her plate with her fork. "A 7.0 on the Richter scale, at the very least," she predicted.

"In case you've forgotten, my grandfather was a construction worker," Althea reminded her pointedly. "And we're talking about you finding someone you are compatible with. Not someone with an acceptable pedigree. Someone you love—not someone handpicked by your father or me."

"I'm sure Daddy would not see it that way," Christina maintained.

Althea was firm. "Your father wouldn't be the one saying 'I do.'"

Joe Parrish.
He did know how to brighten her days. There was yet another letter waiting for her at home that evening. It was almost as if he

knew when she needed to be cheered up and made sure a letter arrived just in the nick of time. He had become so reliable about writing that she could often predict in advance when one of his letters would arrive. She settled down in a large armchair in the oak-paneled book-filled library overlooking the grounds of the Holland estate and carefully opened the envelope...

Dear Christina,
Your photo—the second one—came as quite a relief, especially after the first one. I've never liked women with big hair. The kind a guy's got to be afraid to touch.

And she seems a bit too tall for me.

You wanted a reciprocal photo. Well, I don't have one on hand—guess I'm just not the kind of guy to carry my own picture in my wallet—and it's not at all easy to get film processed here. I asked my mother to send one to me that I could send on to you, but in the meantime a buddy of mine who's a decent artist did a sketch of me. It's a good likeness, I think.

Christina unfolded the drawing he'd enclosed, and when she saw it she started to laugh. She howled with laughter, in fact.

It—and the face in the drawing could only be called an "it"—looked like something from another planet! It resembled a huge tree stump with protruding ears, one huge, bloodshot eye in the center of its hideous head, and lips that could have been Mick Jagger's.

It was the ugliest thing Christina had ever seen.

As you may have guessed, I don't date very often.

You're good, Joe Parrish, Christina thought. You're very good. And I do suppose I deserve it.

Deserve it—and thoroughly enjoy it.

Christina had never flirted with a man in this way before. When she flirted at all, it was always in the most subtle manner possible. She'd never felt free to let her hair down and be so downright silly with a man—certainly not the men she had known. None of them would have found this sort of thing the least bit funny—but, then, they didn't find much of anything funny.

She read on....

For some reason, women aren't wild about guys with one eye. Or maybe it's the ears. Do you think it could be the ears?

What I think, Joseph, is that you're giving me a well-deserved dose of my own medicine, Christina thought, trying not to choke on her own laughter. What I think is that you're enjoying this little exchange as much as I am.

Maybe more so.

What I think is that I like you more than any of the men I've ever known.

What I think is that I must be nuts.

It's good to be able to laugh like this, Christina. I don't know about you, but I need to know there are still things to laugh about. There are days I get pretty depressed here, so far from home, so far from anywhere, it seems. There's nothing but sand, as far as the eye can see. Sand and guys in fatigues who, after a while, all look alike. Not much of a view, believe me. What keeps me going is thinking about happier times, happier things: family get-togethers, weddings, births of new family members, that sort of thing. It's hard for me to believe that our way of life might not appeal to everyone, but I guess that depends on what you happen to be accustomed to.

In college, I dated the daughter of the richest man in my hometown. I should have known better. We had nothing in common. How could we? After all, we came from two very different social backgrounds.

Anyway, I invited her to one of our Sunday dinners. It was a big deal, a special occasion. My brother and his wife had just had their first baby and were bringing her home from the hospital. We were all pretty excited, except my date. She was so bored that she didn't even bother to try to hide it!

I should have realized then that we weren't suited to each other, that it wasn't going to work. I might have saved myself a lot of heartache.

The daughter of the richest man in town... we had nothing in common... I should have realized...

The words ran through Christina's mind like a constant echo. I can imagine what he'd say if he knew his "pen pal" is a senator's daughter who grew up among the Middleburg Horse People, she thought grimly.

I wouldn't have to buy any more stamps.

She never was comfortable in the midst of my big, rowdy family. She sat in the same spot all afternoon, looking like she'd been glued there, with a horribly pained look on her face. She would have been much happier, I'm sure, with her own kind.

Her own kind. My own kind. Christina thought unhappily. Makes us sound like an endangered species. But then, maybe we are, at that.

The more time I spent with her, the more I realized we'd never last. I couldn't give her what she wanted, what she was accustomed to. She would never have wanted—or even tried—to fit into my way of life.

We were doomed before we ever got started.

If anyone else had made that remark, she would have called that person a snob—but somehow, coming from Joe, she couldn't believe it had been intentional. No... he was no doubt trying to be realistic about a relationship that had never stood a chance.

I should know better than to think that I could fit in with the silver-spoon crowd—or vice versa.

Class distinction is a royal pain, Christina thought, frustrated. She hated it when her so-called friends had looked down on those who were less secure financially, and she hated it now. Why, she wondered, did the balance of one's bank account make that person more or less attractive?

And why did the ability to bear children make one woman more desirable than another who couldn't?

> Yes, it's the family that matters most. Especially the children. Nothing makes me remember how precious life is quite as strongly as the birth of a new baby....

The birth of a baby.

Those last words had all of the impact of a bullet through the heart. Christina drew in a deep breath. Children obviously meant a great deal to him. That didn't exactly come as a great surprise. After all, he came from a large, closely knit family. He'd grown up with lots of children around. His brothers and sisters had all started families of their own already. When he went home after his stint in the Gulf, he would once again be surrounded by children.

This was undoubtedly a man who wanted a large family of his own.

Christina was forever reading and hearing about those forward-thinking men who were looking for career women to merge with—women who didn't necessarily want children. Men who supposedly didn't want that kind of responsibility.

But Christina had yet to meet any of them.

She liked this man she'd never met, this Joseph Parrish. Right from the beginning, his letters had reflected the personality of a man who was open and warm, a man who wasn't afraid to *feel*. So unlike myself, she thought as she read further.

> Those memories come in handy here, especially late at night. The nights are six months long here, you know.
>
> I'm only kidding. I think that's the Arctic Circle. But that's how it feels here sometimes. There are nights I lie awake all night, when it's too hot to sleep, just thinking, remembering... thinking about my family back home reminds me how important our work here really is.
>
> It doesn't make it any easier, but it does make it understandable.
>
> I think when they finally do send us home, I'll go into business for myself. I'm going to find a chemist who can invent a shampoo that gets *all* of the sand out of your hair. Or I could get rich

quick by going into the pest-control business. I'd just print up a million of Sergeant Lewis's photo—he's the one who really posed for that sketch I sent you—and sell them for a dollar each. This guy's so ugly it's hard to believe he could live. One look at his ugly kisser would scare *anything* away....

Christina laughed. She often found herself laughing, sometimes quite hysterically, at his letters. He had a delightful sense of humor. It was his humorous observations of his own life and the people who had passed through it that had many times helped Christina forget her own problems. Her own unsolvable problems. He was a man she could care about—someone she could care *too much* about, under the circumstances.

There's no future in this relationship, she had to keep reminding herself.

With her parents out for the evening and the staff having been given the night off, Christina had the house to herself, a rare occurrence. Not that it really mattered to her, one way or the other. She spent the entire evening in her room, reading... and thinking.

Mostly, she was thinking about Joe Parrish.

She liked him, more than any of the men she'd been "officially" involved with. More than she'd ever believed she could like a man she'd only known through his letters. He was so open and honest and without pretense—so different from her former fiancé, Curtis Shellcross IV. So different from the men she'd grown up with, men who were obsessed with status, with "appearances."

He seemed to have only one thing in common with them. One very important thing.

Maybe I'm wrong, she thought, grasping at the last thread of hope available to her. Maybe he's not so crazy about the idea of having lots of children of his own. Just because he loves kids—and he obviously does—doesn't mean he's so set on having his own. Maybe he'd be willing to adopt. Just because he's so fond of his nieces and nephews doesn't mean he'd want a large brood of his own.

But the realist in her knew the odds were against that.

I'm becoming a truly desperate woman, she thought with overwhelming self-disapproval as she automatically put her bookmark in place and closed the book she'd been trying to read. Putting the book down, she got up and went to her desk. She gave a great deal of thought to what she wanted—no, needed—to say before finally putting pen to paper.

Dear Joe,
I'm curious about something...

Chapter Six

They were writing to each other almost every day now. Joe kept all of the letters he received from Christina bundled together with a large rubber band, as he did all of his letters from his mother and Max, to be reread whenever the loneliness became intolerable—which was increasingly often these days.

He was surprised to find that he'd come to know her—or felt that he knew her, at least—as well as he would have known her if they'd grown up together as next-door neighbors. In the course of their correspondence, she'd become more and more open, confiding her feelings and dreams to him. There were times she was very serious....

> When I was young, horses were my life. I once dreamed of riding in the Olympics. In fact, it was all I thought about from the time I was ten years old. But it just wasn't meant to be....

> I know how you must have felt when your dog died. When I was a little girl, I had a dog I loved, too—a little terrier named Trouble. But Trouble was sickly, even as a puppy. When she died, I didn't think I'd ever be able to stop crying....

> I hated being an only child. Sometimes there were other kids around, but mostly I was alone, and I hated being alone. I made up for it by developing a rich fantasy life. You are so lucky to have had brothers and sisters....

My parents always said I was a good child. I suppose it was because that's what was expected of me—and I always did what was expected of me. I was always obedient, yet a part of me longed to be a rebel, to break the rules, to *not* always do what was expected....

And then there were the times she was downright funny:

Maybe I'll buy a motorcycle—a big one with everything on it. That would be fun. And I'd dress in black leather from head to toe. And chains. Definitely chains. Think I could terrorize anyone?

This guy was a real jerk, a grade-*A*, number one, first-class *jerk*. He accused me of holding a gun to his head. Can you believe *that?* I told him if I had a gun to *his* head, I'd pull the trigger!

My father was forever trying to arrange dates for me. He was especially skilled at finding the most boring, arrogant men on the face of the earth. There was one fellow—he had one hundred and one different allergies. This one was so bland that if you put him up against a beige wall, he'd blend in. I had to slap him twice—I thought he was dead!

And then there were her whimsical moments, when she did things that took him completely by surprise—like sending him that Bride of Frankenstein photograph.

Overall, he had come to know her as a woman who was beneath the surface deeply unhappy. No matter how cheerful her letters often were, that underlying sadness was always there, always in evidence. That, he decided, could be the reason she spent so much time writing letters to people she'd never met. Maybe we're better—or safer—than the people she knows in the flesh.

She's a heck of a lot better than the women *I've* known.

That's pretty much the story of my life.
I always somehow manage to attract men with whom I have nothing at all in common.

Welcome to the club, Joe thought, knowing only too well what *that* was like.

I used to think there was something wrong with me, but I finally reached the conclusion that I'd just been sending out the wrong signals to the wrong men—so I voluntarily removed myself from the singles scene for the time being.
At least until I can figure out how not to do whatever it is I've been doing wrong.

If you ever do, tell me, Joe thought. Maybe it'll help me figure out what *I've* been doing wrong!

My best friend's getting married. the man she's marrying is a world-class jerk, but I gave up trying to convince her of that a long time ago. She knows, but chooses not to see it—and probably won't, not until it's too late. He's been cheating on her all along, he doesn't care about anyone but himself.
You probably know the type.

Oh, I know the type, all right, Joe thought. I'm intimately familiar with the female of the species.

Have you ever known anyone like that?

Have I ever known anyone like that? He laughed aloud at the question. Without meeting any of those guys, I know they can't hold a candle to Mindy when it comes to being vain, shallow and self-centered. She was a real prize. But fortunately for Max—and for me—her dominant traits aren't hereditary.

This sounds really sick, doesn't it, Joe?

No, it sounds like you and I have made some of the same wrong turns along the rocky road of romance. In fact, we must've ended up on the same street.

I'm not really so desperate. I'm just discouraged. Good men seem so hard to find these days. Almost impossible, in fact.

Tell me about it. Must be almost as hard as finding a good woman. There aren't many of them living in Indiana. That much I'm sure of.

You seem like a good man, Joe Parrish. You're restoring my faith in the opposite sex.

I could say the same for you, Christina Holland. But the emotional scars Mindy left would not heal quickly.
If ever.

It really surprises me that you're not married.

Surprises you? You should talk to my mother, Joe thought, smiling to himself.
Everyone else in my family married young.

Have you ever been married?

Not even close, he thought. No marriage, no engagement, no serious relationship. I do, however, have a child. Does that count?

> At least we live in a time in which being single past the age of twenty-five doesn't make us freaks.

Joe smiled to himself. Speak for yourself, he thought. But thank you anyway for the vote of confidence, Christina.

A complex lady, he thought. And a most intriguing one.

"If I don't get home soon, I may not have a home to go home to," Dave worried aloud, as he read a letter from his attorneys. "Seems Josie wants the house, the car and half of our savings. She and that jerk she's seeing have probably cleaned out the other half already."

Joe listened but said nothing in response. He had a pretty good idea of how Dave was feeling. He knew how *he'd* feel. He could only imagine what his life would have been like now if he'd married Mindy. Mindy was definitely not the type to sit around waiting for a man—any man—who could be away for a very, very long time. No...not Mindy. She would have found herself a suitable replacement within a week. If it took her that long. Mindy needed a man, but only for attention. Only to feed her insatiable ego.

And maybe, occasionally, to take care of a few other needs.

The longer he was here, the longer he observed the strain military life placed on the marriages of the men he'd come to know and regard as his friends, the more convinced he was that Mindy wasn't an endangered species after all. There were a lot of Mindys in the world. There were a lot of women just like her, all over the U.S.—and probably in a lot of other places, too. And an incredibly large number of them seemed to be married to servicemen.

Maybe I'm lucky to be single after all, he told himself.

Then there were the days, trouble or not, that he found himself wishing that he did have a "significant other" waiting for him back home.

There were the days he wished that, when his tour of duty was over, he could know he would have someone to go home to. Oh, he had Max. He had his mother and the rest of his family. And he loved them all dearly. But it just wasn't the same.

It was love—but not the kind of love he needed at the moment.

Not the kind of love he'd needed for a long time now.

The kind he'd never had.

The kind he'd fantasized about.

The kind he'd begun to fantasize about now, with Christina.

Christina.

This is silly, he told himself. This woman is halfway around the world. We've never even met.

Yet I have more in common with her than I do with any other woman I've ever known.

Stranger things have happened.

But not to me.

Never to me.

Well...I suppose there's a first time for everything.

Even for me.

The letter from Max broke Joe's heart.

Dear Dad,
I saw her today—Mindy, I mean. It

wasn't planned or anything like that. I just ran into her—really ran into her—at the mall. It was like bumping into a total stranger, though she looks just like her photo. She didn't know me at all, and she wasn't friendly.

It felt so weird, Dad. She's my mother, but I don't feel like she's my mother. I don't feel like she's anybody to me. I looked up at her, and it was like she was just another stranger. Just somebody in the crowd.

She is a stranger to you, sport, Joe thought angrily. She may have given birth to you, but she's never been a mother to you.

Never.

From the day he was born, Joe had done everything he could to make it up to Max for never having been able to give him the one thing all children need: a mother. He'd always felt he'd failed his son miserably. Max was a healthy, well-adjusted little boy—but more and more often, Joe was aware that he endured a great deal of emotional anguish as a result of Mindy's indifference toward him. It would have been so much easier if Mindy weren't still in town. Joe wouldn't have had to tell Max everything.

Max was a boy with a lot of love to give and not enough people to give it to—so when he was very young, he'd started giving it to animals. First there had been turtles and lizards. Then the goldfish he'd gotten for his fifth birthday. Then came the hamsters, gerbils and—much to his grandmother's dismay—the mice. After that, the guinea pig. Then there were the doves, Moe, Larry and Curly.

When he was eight years old, Max had announced that he wanted to become a veterinarian. Today, two years later, it was still his goal.

At least he knows what he wants to do with his life, Joe thought. That's more than I can say for myself.

In that two years, Max's surrogate family had grown to include two rabbits who often slept with him and used a litter box just like a cat, an ornery little green parrot who wouldn't allow anyone but Max to touch him, an overweight dachshund with a crabby streak, a black German shepherd who'd been abused by her previous owner, a family of lizards and a rather lively little crayfish who was growing in leaps and bounds.

"Animals love you if you love them," Max explained to his father.

And Joe knew how important that unconditional love was to his son.

How do I tell Christina about Max? Joe asked himself. Do I just say, "Oh, by the way—there's something I forgot to tell you. I have a ten-year-old son?" I guess that's the logical approach, though I'd probably sound like a complete idiot, he told himself.

One doesn't forget to mention that he has a child. Especially when he has sole custody of that child.

No, she'd never believe it. She'd wonder why I didn't tell her.

Unless she's like all the others. Then she'd *know* why. But she wouldn't care. It wouldn't matter to her one way or the other, because I'd never hear from her again.

But Joe couldn't believe she was like that. He didn't *want* to believe it. In her letters she sounded so sensitive, so caring....

Daddy had a heart attack five years ago. The entire time he was in the intensive-care unit, Mother and I rarely left the hospital, and never did we both leave at the same time. We were so afraid he wasn't going to make it. He almost died twice.

I've never been so frightened in my life.

Joe didn't doubt it for a moment. There were tearstains on the pages of that particular letter. He could tell by the writing that her hand must have been trembling. Just the memories of that time in her life had been terribly upsetting for her.

This was a woman who was capable of some very deep emotions.

I blamed myself for the horse's death. I had been riding him at the time. I did something wrong, I'm still not sure what, but I did. He fell and broke his leg. He had to be put down. I think I must have cried for a week. That horse was my baby. I watched the mare give birth to him. I raised him, trained him.

Then, suddenly, he was dead and it was my fault.

I don't know which was more unbearable—the grief or the guilt.

Sounds to me like they were about even in the pain department, Joe thought, having found it all too easy to share her grief.

If she could care so deeply for a horse, surely she had even more love and compassion to give to a child.

Even if she hadn't given birth to that child.

I love Christmas, but it always depresses me. I start out in a good mood when I head out for a day of shopping—then I see the festive decorations and the displays and the children with Santa Claus and zap! I end up depressed.

Why?

You're depressed because during the holidays, even though you've got your folks, it's not the same thing. You're alone, and for whatever reasons, the holidays make all of us who are unattached more acutely aware of that fact.

Believe me. I know.

Joe was still debating telling Christina about Max when her latest letter arrived.

Dear Joe,
I'm curious about something. I've gotten the impression from your letters that you're quite fond of children—but then, that's to be expected, given that you're from such a large, close-knit family. Still, a lot of people love kids but don't want any of their own...

Well, Joe thought, she gave me an opening—and her timing couldn't have been better.

He read that paragraph again. She was asking how he felt about children, but gave no indication as to how *she* felt about them.

Well, there's only one way to find out, he thought, reaching for pen and paper.

He'd just have to ask her.

Dear Christina,
Now that you mention it, I'm a little curious myself...

He shook his head and tore up the page. This was a serious matter. He didn't want to come off sounding flip.

Dear Christina,
You asked how I feel about kids, but you never told me how *you* feel...

He thought about it for a long moment. It wasn't exactly what he wanted to say, but he couldn't seem to come up with a better way to say it.
And this was no time for subtlety.

Chapter Seven

"By the way... I ran into an old friend of yours last night," Daphne announced casually as she stood in front of a mirror at the trendiest boutique in town, holding a blue silk dress up in front of herself to see if the color would look good on her.

Christina, preoccupied with the earrings she was trying on, seemed only remotely interested. "Oh? Who?" she asked.

Daphne, dissatisfied, handed the dress back to the salesgirl. "Curt Shellcross."

Christina frowned. "Curt Shellcross is no friend of mine," she stated flatly. Suddenly the earrings had lost their appeal, too.

"As I recall, *dahling,*" Daphne began in a joking tone, "the dear boy used to be much more than a friend."

"That was before the skunk showed his stripe," Christina said, annoyed. She reached for another pair of earrings.

"And this was the man you had planned to marry?" Daphne giggled.

"That was a long time ago—and if I'd realized then what kind of man he was, I would never have even gone out with him," Christina insisted.

A long time ago... it seemed like another lifetime to Christina, that summer five years ago when she'd been engaged to marry Curtis Buckley Shellcross IV. The Shellcross family was as "old money" as it was possible to be. Christina's father had joked that the Shellcrosses had invented the U.S. dollar, and it wasn't far from the truth. One of the first banks to open in the New World had been opened by a Shellcross.

Christina had grown up with Curt and his sister, Jayne, who was much more down-to-earth than her class-conscious brother. Christina and Curtis had dated in college, and after graduation they'd gotten engaged. It had been a long engagement, with Christina repeatedly putting off setting a wedding date until she could muster the courage to tell Curt about her "problem."

When she could stall no longer, when her mother had planned the wedding of the year and sent out invitations to five hundred of the families' closest friends, Christina finally made her confession. They'd been out to dinner that night with friends, and on the way home she'd told him everything. It was a night she would never be able to forget, she thought ruefully, as she recalled that evening....

"Mother's still trying to find a mother-of-the-groom ensemble that suits her," Curt said, amused. "She's tried every acceptable store between here and Baltimore, and has yet to find a thing she likes. I think she's going to fly up to New York next week."

Christina hadn't responded. She'd been thinking—all evening, in fact—about how she was going to break it to him, how she was going to tell him that if he married her, there would be no Curtis Shellcross V.

"You've been so quiet tonight," Curt observed aloud for the first time. "Are you not feeling well?"

"I'm fine," she assured him. "That is, I'm not ill. Physically." She paused, turning to face him in the darkness of his Mercedes. "Curtis, there's something I have to tell you."

"All right," he responded promptly. "Tell me."

That was Curt. Just spit it out, no matter what it was.

"Stop the car."

He gave her a sideways glance, and she could tell that he was surprised. "All right," he agreed, slowly, pulling the car off to the shoulder of the road. It wasn't a frequently traveled road, and there were few cars on it, especially at that time of night. Curt turned to look at Christina, and even in the darkness he was the most physically attractive man she'd ever seen, with his golden blond hair and pale blue eyes. He looked like a movie star, though such a comparison would have appalled him. "This sounds important."

"It is." Christina frowned. "There's something you have to know about me before we can get married," she started.

He smiled. "Let me guess. You were married before and you've just discovered that the divorce isn't legal, so if we were to marry, you'd be a bigamist.

"This is serious, Curt."

He looked at her, finally concerned, but said nothing, waiting for her to go on.

"Years ago...do you remember when I was in the hospital when we were kids?"

He thought about it for a moment, then nodded. "You fell from your horse. A nasty fall, as I remember."

"Yes. It was." She fumbled for the right words, all the time hoping Curt loved her enough that it wouldn't matter to him, but afraid that family tradition was stronger than love. "There were complications—complications no one knew about at the time."

"I'm afraid I don't understand—"

Get it over with, a voice from somewhere deep within herself screamed. "There was a lot of internal bleeding, a lot of damage. To save my life they had to operate—to do a hysterectomy.''

He looked as though he'd been physically struck. "A hysterectomy? That means—"

She couldn't look him in the eye. "It means I can never have children," she said gravely.

His swift intake of breath told her he was already reconsidering the future of their relationship. "When you drop a bomb, you don't mess around, do you?" he asked finally, shaking his head. He was just as upset as she'd expected him to be.

"I felt you had a right to know."

"How thoughtful of you to get around to telling me now, with the wedding only two weeks away and the invitations already out," he snapped irritably. It was then that she knew there would be no wedding.

She doubted there was any point in discussing it further, but decided she had to, even though she was sure he'd already made up his mind about them. "I suppose you'll want to call off the wedding," she said quietly, looking down at the beaded evening bag that lay in her lap, but not really seeing it.

"Under the circumstances, that shouldn't come as any great surprise," he responded tightly.

"No, of course not," she said, trying to control the anger that was building within her. "After all, I wouldn't be able to keep up my end of the *deal,* now, would I?"

He turned on her venomously. "Now what is that supposed to mean?"

"It means, quite simply, that you never really cared about me at all."

"That's not true—"

"Yes, it is," she cut him off sharply. "If you really loved me, this wouldn't matter to you—but I don't think you really know the meaning of the word! All I am to you—all I've ever been—is a pedigreed brood mare you wanted to acquire, to guarantee the purity of the Shellcross bloodline in future generations. Now that heirs are out of the question, I'm useless as far as you're concerned!"

"My father—"

"I'm not marrying your father, I'm marrying *you*—or I thought I was, until tonight!" she shouted, her eyes brimming with tears. "Maybe I should count my blessings that I'm *not!*" Christina's thoughts returned to the present as Daphne nudged her, trying to get her to look at a pair of pearl earrings. She was still thinking about that night with Curt—how angry she had been, not just with him, but with herself as well for having believed he'd ever really loved her. She hadn't given him the opportunity to finish what he'd been trying to say that night, but she knew what it would have been if she had. He would have told her how his father expected him to provide heirs, sons to carry on the Shellcross name. How it was his responsibility as the only son.

He would not have mentioned love, because love had never really been a part of their relationship. No... it had been, quite simply, a merger between the Holland and Shellcross families, a marriage that would have been made in Fort Knox. Or the Social Register.

It's like something out of the Dark Ages, Christina thought bitterly. Had she not been so miserable, she would have laughed.

If it hadn't been reality—*her* reality—it would have been funny.

That night, she reread some of the letters she'd received from Joe. Thinking about the shallowness of Curtis Shellcross made her appreciate a real man like Joe Parrish all the more. A man who was so different from the man she'd almost married. A marriage that would have been a disaster from the first "I do."

If I ever get out of here, I never want to see sand again as long as I live. It's a good thing I don't live near the beach. Maybe I'll relocate, move to Alaska. An igloo would look pretty good to me right now....

My first job was as a messenger boy. The boss told me up front that there was no room for advancement, but my mother said that was a perfect job for me because I had no ambition. She even offered to write him a letter to that effect....

You know what I'd really like to do? I'd like to be an artist. A real artist, a painter. Of course, my father would say that's not a real job, that artists don't make any money until after they're dead. But then, I could be a B-movie actor. You've seen my portrait. What do you think?

Christina smiled to herself.

Dad always said I was like an old dog who'd been with the same family since I was a puppy—I didn't want to be away from home, not even overnight. As a kid, I only went on family camping trips, much as I loved camping, because I just couldn't stand to be away from my family.
It's hard, even now.

Yes, this is definitely a man who places a great deal of importance on home and family, Christina concluded with an assortment of conflicting emotions. This is a man who probably wants lots of children.
His own children.

Growing up on the farm, it was like living in a dormitory. Our house was large enough, but even so, there were only so many bedrooms. All of the boys were in one bedroom, all of the girls in another. Most of the time, we'd stay awake talking half the night. Other times, we'd fight. Boy, would we fight!

I used to think I hated it—always having to share a bedroom, never having any real privacy—until I had to be away for the first time. Then I was homesick like you wouldn't believe. I missed the house. I missed my family. I even missed the bickering.

I guess that sounds pretty silly, huh?

No, Joe—it doesn't sound silly at all, Christina thought. It sounds like you had a wonderful childhood and just hated to leave it behind.

Sometimes I wish I could have been a child forever, too.

Her own childhood *had* been good. Better than good. It had been so wonderful in so many ways—but growing up an only child had been unbearably lonely most of the time.

And Christina was still lonely.

She could only hope she didn't sound *too* desperate in her letters to Joe. In the beginning, it had been so easy to confide in him—someone she'd never met and wasn't likely ever to meet. He'd seemed to be a warm, caring person, and there had been no emotional attachment between them.

At least not then.

Now, she wasn't so sure.

It seems like every time we all get together back home, we end up rehashing those days in great detail. We can laugh about it now, but it did get pretty hairy sometimes. We—my brothers and I—sometimes wouldn't speak to each other for days at a time.

With the girls it was even worse. They fought among themselves and they fought with us. Mostly, the fighting was over the bathroom. In a household with that many people and only one bathroom, you can imagine what it was like.

No, I can't, Christina thought sadly. But sometimes, most of the time, in fact, I do wish I could.

I wish I knew what living in—or having—a large family was like.

Here I am, rambling on about things that happened years ago—and probably boring you to death.

You could never bore me, Joe Parrish, Christina thought.
Never!

All of my brothers and sisters are married now (please bear with me if I've already told you any of this, Christina—I forget sometimes what I've written from one letter to the next!). They look at me like I'm some kind of oddball. They keep asking, "When are you going to take the plunge?"

How do I make them understand that finding the right woman has been—so far—an impossible task?

If you ever figure that one out, let me know, Christina thought.

I'll probably have to start telling Mother and Daddy something soon myself.

She started to put the letter back in the envelope, then noticed there was something else in there. A photo. She took it out and looked at it, smiling.

Joe.

He was a good-looking man—but more than that, he had a kind face. Compassionate eyes. A warm smile.

It was a good sign.

Another letter was waiting for her when she came home from work the next day, but this was one she wasn't sure she was looking forward to reading. She took it up to her room, where she could do so in privacy.

Dear Christina,
You asked how I feel about kids, but you never told me how you feel about them.

I love kids. I've always loved kids. I'd have a whole houseful of them if I had

> my way—but then, that's the way I grew up, as you said yourself. I'm used to a houseful of kids. I'm used to a houseful of anybody.
>
> I've often thought about how wonderful it would be to have a family of my own one day soon. You know—a wife, kids, a couple of dogs (mongrels, of course—I love mutts), a big, rambling old house that I could buy cheap and fix up myself.
>
> What about you? How do you feel about that sort of thing?

How do I feel? She reread that last line over and over again. *I feel like I've been punched in the stomach, Joe. Hard.*

His response didn't come as a surprise to her—she'd suspected all along that children would be important to him, if not for the same reasons that they'd been important to Curtis Shellcross IV. No, Joe Parrish wanted kids, but he wanted them for all the right reasons. The same reasons she wanted them.

Children she could never have.

It's always the same, she thought miserably.

Christina had come to care a great deal about Joe. She'd looked forward to finally meeting him when the army sent him home. She'd entertained the possibility of having a real relationship with him, had wondered if it was possible.

It wasn't. She was sure of that now.

The more she thought about it, the more certain Christina was that there was no point in prolonging the inevitable. There was no future in it. They were pen pals, to borrow a term from her schoolgirl days. They could even be described as friends. But she knew now that it would never be more than that. At first, she'd thought the best thing for both of them would be for her to just stop writing to him altogether, to cease all contact with him—but she finally had to admit that she liked him too much to do that.

But did she really want to be "just friends"?

She gave it a great deal of thought before even attempting to write him again. Now, sitting at her desk with pen in hand, she blinked back a tear as she started to write...

Dear Joe,
I can't say I was surprised by your last letter...

Chapter Eight

There were times when even the happiest memories were not enough.

This was one of those times, Joe decided as he lay on his cot, on his back, arms folded behind his head, staring up at the vacant emptiness at the top of the tent. He was thinking about what must be going on back home right now. His mother was probably making breakfast. He could almost smell the bacon frying and the biscuits in the oven. His dad was probably out in the fields already, getting in a few hours' work before breakfast—as he almost always did. Max would be feeding his rapidly growing family of pets. And Christina? Joe couldn't even begin to imagine what Christina was doing right now, or where she might be.

What was her home like? Her family? These were things she'd never written about in any of her letters. Oh, she'd mentioned her parents often enough for him to know that she had a good relationship with both of them. But she never really gave him any idea of what her background was. Not that it mattered—he was just curious. He'd never thought she was hiding anything.

But he'd wondered.

He'd always had the feeling, more from what she didn't write than from what she had written, that her background was very different from his. Happy, probably every bit as happy as his had been. Just different.

But for whatever reason, she hadn't been anxious to share it with him.

He wondered if she'd gotten his latest letter yet. Even more important, he wondered how she would respond. How she responded to that letter could have a major impact on his future. His, and his son's.

Max.

Max was always going to be his primary consideration. He had to be. For Joe, it could never be a simple matter of finding a woman he loved and allowing nature to take its course. There would always be Max to think of, and Joe couldn't let his son be hurt any more than he had been already. Mindy had done enough damage for one lifetime.

More than enough.

Joe frowned, recalling a conversation he and his son had on a cold winter morning during feeding time at the Parrish family zoo....

"Need some help?" Joe asked as he entered the barn, wearing jeans and a heavy down-filled parka to shield him from the bitter cold.

Max shook his head. "I'm almost done, Dad, but thanks anyway."

That was the coldest morning in recent memory—fifteen below zero. It had snowed the night before, and Joe and Max had had a major difference of opinion over whether or not Max's two rabbits—a male wild rabbit and a young female Dutch—should spend the night in Max's bedroom. Joe thought he'd won the debate—until he'd gone to look in on Max before turning in himself and had found both rabbits in bed with Max. He'd decided not to make an issue of it. Max loved his pets, showering them with all of the love he wasn't able to give his mother.

Joe watched as he cradled the wild rabbit, Bugsme, in his arms. Max had rescued the rabbit, as a baby with barely any fur, from the jaws of one of the Parrish dogs and had raised him as a pet. The rabbit adored the boy. Bugsme, Max had repeatedly explained, had grown up in a way that made him unable to understand that he was wild. Joe suspected the little beast didn't even know he was a rabbit.

"They do seem to like you," Joe observed as Max put Bugsme back in his cage and took out Babs, a chubby brown-and-white Dutch rabbit he claimed to have named for a girl in his class at school.

"Animals love you if you love them," Max said simply. Babs snuggled against him affectionately, finding warmth in his ski jacket. "Like Babs here. She thrives on love."

So do you, son, Joe thought, but didn't share his feelings with Max. It's unfair that you should have been born to such a cold, unfeeling mother.

Joe lay there in the darkness of his tent, thinking about Max and how Mindy had cruelly cheated him. Joe would never forget the day Mindy told him she was pregnant....

"We have a problem," Mindy announced without so much as a hello-how-are-you as she slid into the booth across from him at the diner in town.

"Problem?" Joe tried not to laugh. To Mindy, having the cleaners dye her dress the wrong color to match her new shoes was a problem. Maybe her favorite nail polish had been taken off the market. "Whatever it is, I'm sure it can be easily taken care of," he attempted to calm her.

"Oh, I'm sure it can, but it's such a bother." She paused to flip her long, dark hair off her shoulder. "I'm pregnant."

Joe's head jerked up. "Are you serious?"

"You know me well enough to know I would not joke about such a horrible thing," Mindy pouted.

"How far along are you?" Joe wanted to know.

"Six weeks. An abortion should be quite simple at this point—but we'll have to do it right away."

"An abortion?" Joe hadn't been able to hide the shock and revulsion he felt.

"Well, of course." Mindy drew back and looked at him for a long moment. "You don't expect me to actually have a baby, do you?"

"Well—yes. I thought that might be the natural conclusion—"

Her laugh was hollow. "Oh, come now, Joseph. I can't have a baby now. I don't want to have a baby. This is just one of those unfortunate accidents—they happen all the time."

"Not to me, they don't," he said sharply. "This is my baby, too—but you seem to have decided his future all by yourself."

"It's my body, and I don't want to carry *it!*" she shot back at him.

"You should have thought of that before you got pregnant." He couldn't think of anything else to say. He hadn't been prepared for this.

"It takes two to tango, honey," she responded in an acid tone. "And you didn't use anything, remember?"

"Mindy, don't do anything rash." Arguing with her did no good, so he tried to pacify her in an attempt to keep her from doing anything about the pregnancy until he'd had time to think about it, to come up with an alternative that would satisfy both of them.

"I'm not doing anything rash. I gave this a lot of thought even before it happened. I am not going to have a baby. Not now, not ever."

"We could get married." God, what am I saying? he wondered. I don't want to marry her!

"Don't be silly, Joseph. It's been fun, but I'm not ready to get married—and even if I were, I certainly wouldn't marry you."

He stared at her as though she'd just slapped him, unable to respond.

"You didn't think there was any kind of a future for us, did you?" She obviously found the notion funny, because she laughed at the prospect. "I adore you, honey, but I just can't see myself married to a farmer. It's beneath me!"

"Then don't. Just have the baby and give him to me." Joe wasn't sure the words had actually come from him, but there was no turning back now. "I don't want to marry you any more than you want to marry me—but I want my baby. I'll raise him myself—without you."

She had laughed at him. "Oh, Joseph, you always were an idealist!" She blew him a kiss as she got to her feet and walked out of the restaurant.

It had been all he could do to keep Mindy out of that abortion clinic in Indianapolis. She'd finally agreed to his suggestion, but she had been impossible throughout her entire pregnancy. She hated the idea of losing her figure. She couldn't abide morning sickness. Her swelling feet annoyed her. She couldn't find any maternity clothes that she liked.

Joe was plagued by those unpleasant memories until he finally drifted off into a restless and troubled sleep.

The letter from his mother, which arrived the next day, did nothing to put his mind at ease:

Dear Joe,
I'm worried about Max.

Before you jump to conclusions, he's not ill. That boy is the healthiest child I've ever seen, physically, and his schoolwork isn't suffering—but *he* is. He's having problems, Joseph. Seems he's been getting into a lot of fights lately. He won't talk about it, but his teacher tells me he's been the target of some name-calling. You know how cruel kids can be, and they hear their parents talk....

I know how they talk, all right, Joe thought bitterly. I should have taken him and moved away from there when he was still a baby. I should have taken him somewhere where nobody knew about Mindy and me. I should have let the world—and Max—believe his mother was dead.

That had been his original plan. He'd decided to leave town with the baby as soon as he was born and go somewhere where no one knew them. He'd be a widower whose wife had died in childbirth. No one would be the wiser. That way, if Mindy ever changed her mind and wanted the baby back, she wouldn't be able to find them.

He'd changed his mind and stayed, when he realized there was no way she was ever going to want the baby back. It had been a mistake. He should have gone ahead with his plan.

It would have been painful for Max, Joe thought now, but not nearly as hard to live with as the knowledge that his mother had never wanted him.

It seemed to Joe that it had been, quite literally, forever since he'd sent that last letter off to Christina. How long would it be before he received her response?

And *how* would she respond?

He wondered mostly about that. He wondered about it a lot. He could have told himself he was worrying for nothing, that his concerns were without valid reason—but past experience made it impossible for him to believe that he didn't have every reason in the world to be worried.

He'd been through it all before.

Sometimes, when it started to really get to him, he would reread some of the letters she'd written him over the past months, trying to figure out how she felt, what she was thinking. Once in a while, he found clues.

But most of the time, he didn't.

When I was little, my father used to call me Cinderella. He told me that I was a princess and one day I'd meet a prince and fall in love and live happily ever after.

So far, I've just met a lot of frogs.

She never loses her sense of humor, no matter what, Joe decided. Or is she just laughing to keep from crying, like I am?

Frogs are all right, mind you. Frogs are great, in fact, if you happen to be a high-school biology teacher or you're into the preservation of wildlife. But I don't fit any of those categories. I'm not anti-frog. I just can't bring myself to kiss any of them, that's all.

Now that's definitely a relief. A woman who's into kissing frogs has major league problems!

Even a prince wouldn't make it worthwhile.

Joe laughed aloud at the thought. "I can see that," he said agreeably.

Oh, well. I stopped believing in fairy tales a long time ago.

"Me, too," Joe muttered, nodding as he read. "Me, too."

I've reached the conclusion that Prince Charming just doesn't exist in the real world.

Joe nodded again. "Neither does Cinderella or Sleeping Beauty, honey," he said.

In fact, I'm starting to have serious doubts about "happily ever after" as well.

"I've been wondering about that one myself," Joe admitted, though he would never have said so to anyone who mattered.

There I go again.

"There *I* go again." If this weren't happening to him, he'd probably think it was funny. "You and I, Christina, have a great deal in common. We both sound like truly miserable people."

If they weren't so far apart, they could probably console each other.

Things went from bad to worse when Christina's letter arrived.

Dear Joe,
I can't say I was surprised by your last letter. I had you pegged all along as the kind of man who would want a dozen kids and an equal number of pets, all living in a wonderful kind of chaos in a big, old house with a white picket fence and a tree house and a tire swing in the backyard. I'll bet you'd want a station wagon, too.

To answer your question, I think children are wonderful—but having children of my own just isn't in the cards, unfortunately. I've had to invest a lot of time and energy in my career over the past few years, at first believing that eventually I'd be able to slow down and live a normal life. But now—now I find that the more successful I become, the more demanding and time-consuming my work becomes. It wouldn't be fair of me to have children and not be able to give them one hundred percent.

You probably won't be hearing from me so often in the weeks to come. My work load is such right now that I have little time to call my own....

A kiss-off if I ever heard one, Joe thought bitterly, not bothering to finish reading the letter right then. Well, I had to know...and now I do. She couldn't have made it any clearer if she'd spelled it out in neon lights.

I thought she was going to be different. I was wrong. She's just like all the others.

Chapter Nine

The letter from Joe's mother took Christina completely by surprise.

The letter was quite friendly and informal, sounding as if it had come from an old and dear friend rather than someone she'd never met.

And since I'll be in the area. Anyway, I thought we might meet at last. Joe's told me so much about you. Would you be free for lunch? My son thinks you're pretty special, and I get the feeling that some things he hasn't told you about himself are creating problems for the two of you. I hope that when we meet, I can correct the problem for him...for both of you....

That last line aroused Christina's curiosity. What could Irene Parrish possibly have to tell her that might make a difference as far as she and Joe were concerned? Theirs was a problem for which there was no solution. In spite of her growing love for Joe, she was sure nothing his mother could say or do would make a future for the two of them together a possibility.

Still... the feeling was there.

And she *was* curious.

There was a phone number at the end of the letter. Christina reached for the phone to call, then abruptly changed her mind. She thought about it for a moment, then reached for the phone again. This time, she started to dial, but stopped before completing the number and replaced the receiver.

What's the point? she asked herself.

The point, you idiot, is that you're in love with him. There—she admitted it. She was madly in love with Joseph Parrish.

But there's no future in it. Not when he finds out you can't give him the children he so obviously wants.

You should be used to it. This isn't exactly the first time.

But it is the first time you've really been in love.

The first time it's been so important to you.

She picked up the phone again—and dialed. This time, she didn't hang up.

A woman's voice answered on the third ring. "Hello?"

"Mrs. Parrish?" Christina asked hesitantly.

"Yes."

"This is Christina Holland."

"Oh—yes, dear." The voice on the other end became immediately friendlier. "I take it you got my letter?" she asked.

"It came today," Christina answered, still feeling somewhat awkward.

"Will you be able to meet me?" Mrs. Parrish wanted to know.

Christina drew in her breath. "Not only able, but looking forward to it," she assured the other woman. "If you'll tell me where you're staying and what day is best for you, I can make a reservation...."

Christina put aside the file she'd been reviewing and looked at her watch, as she had every fifteen minutes for the past two hours. Twenty minutes. In another twenty minutes she would be meeting Joe's mother. Mrs. Parrish had called her that morning to ask that she make the lunch reservation for three people instead of two, leaving Christina puzzled. Christina couldn't help wondering who she might be bringing along. She knew it wasn't Joe—he was still in Saudi Arabia.

Who, then?

I guess I'll know the answer in another twenty minutes, she told herself.

She felt like a new bride about to meet her mother-in-law for the first time.

That's ridiculous, she scolded herself. I've never even met Joe. Why should I be so nervous about meeting his mother?

And whoever she had brought with her?

But she was.

She buzzed her secretary. "I'm leaving now, Melissa," she said. "I have a luncheon appointment—and this is one meeting I don't want to be late for."

"So I've noticed."

"I'll be back in a couple of hours—I think," she said with a degree of uncertainty.

"Sure, Chris."

She made one stop before leaving the building. She went to the ladies' room to inspect her appearance in front of the full-length mirror. When she was satisfied that she did indeed look presentable, she proceeded to walk to the restaurant.

She saw the protesters as soon as she turned the corner. They were the last holdouts of the antiwar protesters who'd demonstrated so forcefully against the U.S. involvement in the Gulf. There were maybe fifty of them, all armed with large, crudely lettered signs, marching in front of the government building two blocks from her office. There was a TV crew taping the event, for the evening news, no doubt, and two photographers on the sidelines snapping pictures, probably for the local newspapers.

Christina shook her head as she walked on. What a difference of opinion! She was thinking about all of the men and women stationed in the Middle East, thousands of miles from home, missing their families and the comforts of home as part of a peacekeeping effort.

It always struck Christina as interesting that while one group of people was passionately for something, there was another group that was passionately opposed.

When she reached the restaurant, the hostess informed her that the rest of her party had not yet arrived. Good, she thought as the hostess escorted her to her table. She had wanted to be the first to arrive.

"Would you like a drink, Ms. Holland?" the hostess asked pleasantly.

"Yes, Judy—I think I'll have the usual."

"White wine spritzer, coming up."

Then Christina abruptly changed her mind. "No, Judy—better make it iced tea."

The hostess tried to hide her surprise. "Yes, Ms. Holland."

Wouldn't do to make a bad impression now, would it? Christina asked herself as she sat down and waited for Irene Parrish to arrive. She guessed from what Joe had told her about his family that his mother not only did not drink, but did not approve of anyone else doing so.

"Ms. Holland?"

At the sound of the hostess's voice, Christina looked up. Judy had returned, this time accompanied by a conservatively dressed older woman—and a child, a boy who appeared to be maybe nine or ten years old. Twelve at the most. Probably one of Joe's nephews, Christina decided.

She rose to her feet as the other woman extended her hand. "Irene Parrish," the woman introduced herself. "And this is Max—Joe's son."

Son!

Christina could feel the color draining from her face. She sank back into her chair. Joe had a son? "It's good to finally meet you—both," was all she could manage for the moment.

Irene sat down, and the boy took a seat between them. He looked very much like his father, Christina thought, mentally comparing him to the photo of Joe she had at home—the one he'd finally sent her a few weeks before she'd moved to end their relationship.

"How old are you, Max?" she asked then.

He wasn't the least bit shy. "Ten," he told her, "but my grandma says I'm ten going on forty."

Christina smiled. He would be an easy child to like, once she'd recovered from the shock of discovering Joe had a son. "You're a lot like your father," she told him.

He looked surprised at that comment. "Do you know my dad?"

"In a way."

He nodded as if accepting that. "Grandma says I'm exactly like him."

Christina's eyes met Irene's. "I thought it was time you and Max met," Irene said.

Christina wasn't quite sure she understood, but Irene went on to explain.

"I know Joe didn't tell you certain—things," she said, trying not to tell her in front of the child that Joe had not told her of his existence.

Christina hesitated momentarily. "No... he didn't," she finally admitted.

Irene turned to Max again. "You shouldn't have left the window down on the way over here," she told him. "I think you'd better go to the men's room and do something about your hair. You look like you just got out of bed."

"But, Grandma—" he began in protest.

"*Now,* Max—and wash your hands while you're at it," she said firmly.

"All right," he droned, as he got up and headed toward the back of the restaurant.

After he was gone, Irene turned to Christina again. "Joe was never married to Max's mother—I'm sure you are wondering about that," she said quietly.

Christina nodded.

"Max's mother was not the maternal type. She wasn't the domestic type at all," Irene recalled. "Mindy Purcell was—and still is—a very beautiful woman. But her beauty was entirely on the surface. She was the most vain, unemotional woman I've ever had the misfortune to meet. Joe was so infatuated with her—but he was young and his head was easily turned back then. When she found she was pregnant she wanted to have an abortion, but Joe talked her into having the baby and letting him assume full custody. He's done a fine job of raising Max alone, I think."

Christina gave her a knowing smile. "I suspect he had some experienced help."

Irene smiled, too. "I tried. But make no mistake about it, Joe's been a good father. A full-time father, until he went to the Gulf."

"I'm sure." Christina was thinking of the things Joe had written in his letters about the importance of home and family.

"It hasn't been easy for him," Irene was saying. "He wants very much to settle down and get married, make a real home for himself and Max—but the women he's known haven't been willing to accept another woman's child. They want their own."

"I can't imagine why it should make a difference," Christina said honestly. She would have been more than happy to raise Joe's son as her own—

Then it hit her.

The realization made her smile. *This* was why Joe had dropped all of those not-so-subtle hints about settling down, starting a family. He'd been trying to find out how she'd feel about being a mother to Max! She felt a rush of overwhelming relief course through her.

He already had a child. A child who needed a mother. And Christina needed a child. Maybe it didn't matter to Joe whether or not she could have children, after all.

"I can't tell you what a pleasure it is to finally meet you, Mrs. Parrish," Christina said aloud.

"Irene," the other woman said, smiling.

She smiled. "Irene."

Irene Parrish would never know just how much her visit had meant to Christina. But Christina had a feeling she could guess.

Christina thought about it as she walked back to her office. It had been a much more pleasant afternoon than she'd anticipated. No...it had been more than that. It had changed everything for her.

Irene Parrish had given her something she'd thought was lost forever: hope.

Throughout lunch, Christina had the feeling that Joe's mother had sought her out with a mission in mind. She had not just been "in the neighborhood." Had Joe told her about their relationship, about the turn it had taken when the subject of children came up? Irene had said she knew Joe hadn't told Christina about Max. What else did she know? What else had he told her?

None of that mattered now. All that was important was that Christina knew where Joe had been coming from when he wrote so long and passionately about his desire for a family of his own. He'd wanted to know—no, *needed* to know—how she felt about it, before telling her about his son. She tried to imagine what it must have been like for Joe, being repeatedly rejected by the women he'd cared about because they either didn't want children or wanted only children of their own. She tried to imagine what it must have been like for Max, having been rejected not only by those women, but by his own mother.

Her heart went out to the boy. He seemed like such a good kid. A surprisingly well-adjusted kid, given the kind of mother he'd had. He was everything that Christina would have hoped for in a child of her own. She would have considered herself blessed to have a son like him.

The more she thought about it, the more she wondered if she could one day be a mother to him.

That evening, Christina had dinner alone in her room. Curled up in a large chair in front of the TV but too distracted to watch it, she picked at her food and remembered the things she and Irene Parrish had talked about that day over lunch....

Joe's always been a sensitive boy—man. Mindy's attitude toward him—and especially toward Max—wounded him very deeply. I don't think he ever really got over it....

Oh, there have been other women—but none of those relationships ever worked out, either. The women Joe knew just weren't interested in the idea of raising another woman's child. They all wanted children, but they wanted their own....

Christina wondered if it was too late for them, if she could possibly repair the damage she was sure would have been done by her last letter, if he'd received it by now.

And she was certain he had.

She looked for the answers in the letters he'd already written her.

> I know how you feel. I've known a few toads myself. My most "significant" relationship (and I use the word "significant" in the loosest possible sense!) was with a woman who was more in love with herself than she could ever possibly be with any man.
> That may sound like sour grapes to you, but I swear, with God as my witness, it's true. She really was like that. She didn't want a husband, and she sure didn't want kids. What she wanted, without question, was the total and unrestricted pursuit of her own desires. Her own *selfish* desires. A husband, a family, didn't fit into the plans she'd made for herself.
> Now, I know all women aren't like her, thank goodness, but even so, I've been pretty unlucky in love, no matter who I've been involved with. I guess it's all made me a little gun-shy....

Welcome to the club, Christina thought grimly as she looked up from the page momentarily.

> Still, I keep hoping. I try not to stop believing that, somewhere out there, there's a woman who'll want me *and* all of the things I want, all of the things I grew up with and, for a time, took for granted.
> A woman who will want a family as much as I do.

Christina frowned. Just what she hadn't wanted to hear.
But exactly what she'd *expected* to hear. Or read.

> Most men want a woman who's just like their mothers. I'm no exception. Trouble is, I've yet to meet a woman who fits the bill.

That made Christina smile. She had always said she wanted a man who would be just like her father.

She'd also always said she'd never find one.

Do you think there's any basis in truth to that old myth?

Christina smiled to herself. "I'm beginning to wonder," she said without realizing she'd said it aloud.

Christina wrote to Joe that night:

Dear Joe,
You'll never guess who came to see me today....

No...that sounded corny. She wadded the paper into the smallest ball possible and deposited it into the wastebasket. Besides, he could have known about his mother's plans to look her up.

I met your mother today. I also met your son.

Rather blunt, she thought with a twinge of disapproval. Where do I go from there?

She thought about it for a moment, then started to write again:

> You must be very proud of Max. I know I would be if he were mine.

Not enough, Christina thought. Any woman could find a child "cute" or "captivating" or whatever, without being willing to consider taking on the role of stepmother. She couldn't just say "if he were mine." That had been the problem with the other women in his life.

> Having met both of them, having spent time with them, talked to them, I know now why you wrote the things you did in your letters.
> I will never be able to understand why or how his mother could have turned her back on him as she did. Or how the others could have. *I wouldn't*.

That last part was most important. That was why she'd underscored it. She had to let him know how much she cared, how much she wanted to be a mother to his son as well as a wife to him—if he wanted her.

If he wanted her.

I love you, Joe.

There, she thought, exhilarated. I've said it.

I know I could grow to love Max, Joe, given the chance. Because he's your son, yes, but also because he's a great kid, no matter who his father is....

She paused. There was so much more she wanted to say, yet she couldn't quite find the right words. Why did it always seem that the deeper one had to reach into the heart, the harder it was to find words to express it?

There was so much she wanted to say, needed to say, but a part of her wondered if she might not be too late. When she reached for her pen again, she could think of only one thing to write.

Can you ever forgive me?

Chapter Ten

When Joe received Christina's latest letter, he wasn't sure if he wanted to open it or not.

He expected it to be negative, given the tone of her last letter. He was sorely tempted to open the letter from his mother first—but his curiosity won out, and he tore open the envelope from Christina first. He was glad he did.

Dear Joe,
I met your mother today. I also met your son.

She met Mom—and Max? Joe was stunned. How? Why? Then he remembered. He'd written his mother about his attempts to feel out Christina on her position on children and ready-made families before telling her about his son.

Bless her heart, he thought. He should wring her neck, but he couldn't be angry with her. She'd made that trip to Virginia just to see Christina—as far as he knew, she'd never had any relatives living there, as she'd apparently told Christina she had—to clear the air between them.

He read on.

> You must be very proud of Max. I would be if he were mine....

I am, Joe thought, encouraged by the feeling that she genuinely liked his son.

But then, so had some of the others. They just hadn't liked him enough to want to be a mother to him.

> Having met both of them, having spent time with them, talked to them, I know

now why you wrote the things you did in your letters.

I will never be able to understand why or how his mother could turn her back on him—or how those other women could. *I wouldn't.*

Geez, Mom—how much did you tell her about my past love life? he wondered, stifling a chuckle.

He read that last line again: *I wouldn't.*

He knew then what Christina was trying to tell him. She not only liked Max, she could accept him. She was saying she could not only be a wife to Joe, she could be the mother Max had never had. Joe had never been happier than he was at this moment—and he'd never loved a woman more than he loved Christina.

He continued to read, his vision blurred by the tears he hadn't shed since the day he held his son for the first time:

I love you, Joe.

I love you, too, babe, Joe thought, overcome by a happiness he'd never believed possible.

I know I could grow to love Max, too, given the opportunity. Because he's your son, of course, but also because he's a great kid.

You're both pretty terrific, Joe thought. More than terrific.

Can you ever forgive me?

Forgive you? He wanted to laugh and cry at the same time. Forgive you for *what?*

I have a confession to make, Joe, and once I've made it, I think you'll understand why I reacted as I did to your last letter. You see, when you went on and on about how much having a family meant to you, how much you love children, I didn't know you were already a father. I just thought you were trying to tell me how much you looked forward to having children of your own.

I can't have children, Joe. Not now, not ever.

There was an accident—a long time ago. I fell from a horse and was badly injured. There was a great deal of internal bleeding. An operation was necessary—one that left me unable to have children.

Just as you've encountered women who are unable to accept you and Max as a package deal, the men I've known have always turned away from me when they learned of my inadequacy.

No wonder she reacted the way she did to my letter, Joe thought with a mixture of sadness and anger. She's really been raked over the coals.

There's something else I'd better tell you, as long as I'm confessing.

I haven't been completely honest with you about myself and my background.

It's not that I've lied to you, Joe—I just haven't told you everything, which I suppose is almost as bad. I do work at a PR firm. That much is true. But I don't have to—work, I mean. My family is very wealthy. My father is a senator.

I do have the pickup truck I told you about—but I also have a Maserati. Do you understand what I'm saying?
Can you forgive me?

I already have, Joe thought. He had been a little unnerved by the news that she was rich, that she came from a political background, but he was glad she hadn't told him before now. Not that it mattered to him. It didn't, not really. But he didn't want her to think he'd ever been interested in her only for her money.

She'd probably kept quiet about it for precisely the same reason.

Due to an unexpected visit from the World's Ugliest Living (Alleged) Human Being, also known as Sergeant Lewis, Joe didn't get around to reading his mother's letter until later that evening.

Dear Joe,
I hope you won't be too angry with me, but I went to see Christina, and I took Max with me.

I was only trying to help. I know how much she means to you, and when you wrote that there were problems, that you hadn't been able to find the right way to tell her about Max, well, I thought I could help. I wrote to her. I told her I was going to be in the area visiting relatives (yes, I know we have no family in that part of the country) and would like to meet her.

She's a lovely girl, Joe—everything you said she was and more. And beautiful—I know you've never seen her in the flesh, but she's really quite beautiful. She seems to like Max, and he likes her. I don't think it bothers her at all that you have a son—though I could see that it did come as a surprise to her.

If you're as smart as I think you are, Joseph, you'll hold on to this girl.

I haven't always been smart in the past, Mom, he thought, but I'm learning fast.

And I do intend to hold on to her—somehow.

We spent the afternoon with her. She's a very poised, sophisticated woman—seems to know all the best places in town. The restaurant she took us to was pretty fancy—I would have felt too self-conscious to eat if Christina hadn't gone out of her way to put me at ease. And Max. Max adores her, Joe. It was love at first sight between those two.

I was so proud of Max. Not once did he engage in any of his usual acts of sabotage.

Joe smiled. Max had a sixth sense, when it came to the women in his dad's life. Max knew when they didn't like him, no matter how hard they tried to hide it. He also had a gift for making them miserable once he saw through them.

He must have realized, as Joe had before him, that Christina was something special.

"My luck," Dave complained, pulling off his T-shirt as he crossed the tent to his cot. "One of the few times in my life I'd like to get really and truly stinking drunk, and here I am, stuck in a dry country with no booze for maybe a thousand miles." He flopped down on the cot, disgusted.

"What's the momentous occasion this time?" Joe asked, only half attentive. For the past hour, he'd been trying to write a letter to Christina—without success. He'd started it fifteen times at last count. He knew what he felt, he knew what he wanted to tell her—he just didn't know how to put it into words.

"My divorce becomes final today."

"You've known it was coming for some time now," Joe pointed out with a total lack of diplomacy.

Dave sucked in his breath. "Yeah, I guess." He paused thoughtfully. "I guess a part of me never thought she'd actually go through with it."

Joe stopped what he was doing and shifted around in his chair to face his friend. He personally believed Dave was better off without Josie, but it was pointless to say that to someone—even a good friend—when that friend was still in love with the soon-to-be former spouse. A spouse he loved, no matter how badly she'd treated him.

Joe knew, because he'd been in that boat himself in the past.

"You did what you could, Dave," Joe reminded him. "You made every possible effort under the circumstances to save your marriage—but it takes two, pal, and Josie didn't want to tango."

"Don't you think I know that?" Dave snapped irritably. Hauling himself to his feet, he grabbed a fresh T-shirt and stormed out of the tent.

Joe shook his head, not surprised by his friend's abrupt change of mood. He knew only too well what the pain of a failed relationship was like. But in the past few minutes, he'd also made a new discovery. In the past, witnessing the difficulties his buddies experienced with their wives or girlfriends while stationed in the Gulf had made him skeptical, even gun-shy where women were concerned. But now, just now with Dave—Joe hadn't had even a moment of doubt for himself and Christina.

No more doubts, he thought as he put pen to paper once again. None whatsoever.

At midnight, Joe was still awake. He was still thinking about the letter to Christina had yet not completed. Why was this letter so much harder to write than the others had been? He'd never been more sure of his feelings in his life—yet he was unable to transfer those feelings from his mind, his *heart*, to a sheet of paper.

He loved her—now more than ever. He wanted to tell her that. He *had* to tell her that. That, and so much more. But the words just wouldn't come. He wished he could phone her—but what would he say if he could? If he couldn't write the words, what made him think he could speak them?

Frustrated, he got up and reached for his pad and pen. He started to write....

Dear Christina,
I don't know how the poets do it. How do they express such profound emotion so eloquently?

That sounds dopey, he thought, ripping the page from the pad. He started to throw it away, but then, thinking that even in the trash can someone might see it, he first tore it into a large number of very tiny pieces before disposing of it.

If any of the guys were to read *that*, they'd embarrass him to death. Can't take any chances, he thought as he started to write again.

Dear Christina,
There's so much I want to say to you—but I just can't seem to find the right words.

This is getting me nowhere fast, he thought, growing more annoyed by the minute.

Dear Christina,
I don't quite know how to begin...

As he ripped up yet another unsatisfactory page, the realization came to him. He was going about this all wrong. There was really only one way to say what he was trying to say to her.

Dear Christina,
I love you.

Chapter Eleven

Driving home in unusually heavy traffic, Christina mentally counted the days since she mailed her last letter to Joe. He surely must have gotten it by now. As she had at least a dozen other times in the past week, she wondered how long it would be before he responded.

If he responded.

And if he did... *how* would he respond?

She tried to be optimistic. She told herself she'd said and done all the right things this time, that she'd corrected the mistakes she'd made before.

But was it too late?

Some people couldn't forgive. Sometimes it was impossible to forget.

Had her attempts to make amends come too late for Joe, for them?

Think positive, she kept telling herself. You have to think positive.

She had to believe he still cared.

Halfway around the world, Joe was counting the days.

Did she get my letter? he wondered anxiously. If she did, what will her answer be?

He never would have believed it possible. Six months ago, if anyone had told him he'd propose—by mail, no less—to a woman he'd never even met, he would have laughed in that person's face. But, then, six months ago he wouldn't have believed he'd be proposing to any woman in the immediate future. Six months ago, he didn't believe Ms. Right existed.

At least not for him.

But she did exist. And her name was Christina Holland.

How long will it take? he asked himself as he stared into the star-filled night sky and wondered if she was looking at the same stars. God, that was corny. Like something out of an old movie. I'm living all of the old clichés!

Did she have the letter? Had she already sent off her answer?

Her family. Her father was a U.S. senator. How would he feel about his only daughter marrying an enlisted man? How would Senator Holland feel about his daughter marrying a man who wasn't able to keep her in the manner to which she was undoubtedly accustomed?

Would it matter to her if they did?

Maybe he shouldn't have sent the letter.

Maybe he shouldn't have even written it.

Maybe he should have thought it over before he wrote.

He'd probably made a big fool of himself.

Why would she want to marry someone like him?

Still ... she had said that she loved him.

He had to believe she'd meant it.

Parrish, you're thinking like an idiot, he scolded himself. Idiot or not, the waiting was going to kill him.

The minute she got in the door, Christina went straight to the bronze dish in the entry hall where Marnie always left the day's mail. Joe's letter was on the top of the stack, almost as if Marnie had known Christina would be the first one home that day and would be looking for it.

Christina snatched it up and ripped it open. The note inside was short and very much to the point:

Dear Christina,
I love you. Will you marry me?
                 All my love always,
                     Joe

"Will I marry you?" Christina asked aloud. She thought her heart was going to burst. She thought it was going to stop. She was laughing and crying at the same time, unable to believe it, even though it was right there in front of her in black-and-white.

He wanted to marry her!

She wanted to tell someone, anyone. She *had* to tell someone. She had to tell someone quickly or she would burst. "Mom?" she called out.

No answer.

"Mom!"

Still no answer.

"Daddy?"

No response.

"Daddy?"

Nothing.

"Marnie?"

Again, no answer.

"Is anybody home?" she shouted at the top of her lungs.

Nothing still.

Terrific, she thought, frustrated. When I want someone to be around, no one is.

She looked down at the letter in her hand again. *I love you. Will you marry me?*

She was fighting back tears of joy as she read it again and again. "Will I marry you?" she asked aloud. "You bet your boots I will!"

She wondered if her father could possibly manage an act of Congress to get him home by Thursday.

* * *

Maybe I should call her, Joe thought. The suspense was killing him.

Yeah, right—like I can just pick up a phone anywhere in the desert and call her like I'd make a phone call across town back home.

But, then, there were ways. It wasn't easy most of the time, but it was possible.

If one could be patient and if one were willing to fight through a Mount Everest of red tape, it could be done.

Right now, he decided, anything would be better than just waiting.

I should call him, Christina thought, pacing the floor in the library until she'd practically worn a path in the carpet. I should give him my answer before I tell anyone else.

But how?

How do I get a call through to him?

Getting a call through to anyone stationed in the Gulf wasn't the easiest thing in the world to do. One had to go through certain appropriate channels.

Unless...

She could ask her father. He could get a call through for her.

She phoned his office. "Tracy, this is Christina Holland. Is my father in?" she asked.

"Sorry, Ms. Holland," the voice on the other end responded. "He just left."

"Oh." She hesitated momentarily. "He's on his way home, then?"

"I doubt it," Tracy said. "He had a meeting outside the office. He said he expected to be late."

Great, Christina thought.

"Is something wrong?" Tracy asked. "I can try to track him down for you—"

"No, Tracy—thank you, anyway," Christina declined her offer, even though she was sorely tempted to take her up on it.

"Are you sure?"

"Yes. I'm sure."

"If you change your mind—"

"I won't. Everything's fine," she insisted.

Or it would be, soon.

"How easy is it to get a call through to the States?" Joe asked Dave.

"About as easy as it was for E.T. to phone home," Dave answered in a slightly sarcastic tone. He'd been walking around with a chip on his shoulder the size of the Rock of Gibraltar ever since his divorce became final.

"Who do I see about it?" Joe pursued, unwilling to give up.

"What?"

"About making a call to the States! Dave, you haven't heard a word I've said," Joe said accusingly.

"Sure I have," Dave responded absently.

Joe looked skeptical. "Sure you have."

"Okay so I *was* a little distracted," Dave admitted irritably. "What did you say?"

"I asked who I should talk to about placing a call to the States," Joe repeated, losing patience with his buddy fast.

"The guy to see," Dave began with a sadistic note in his voice, "is none other than your friend and mine, Sergeant Lewis. Now—do you still want to go for it?"

Joe didn't answer right away. Why did it have to be Lewis?

"Daddy, I need your help."

Winthrop Holland looked at his daughter, wondering if there was cause to be concerned. He'd never seen his daughter so full of anxiety. "Of course, honey," he answered in a reassuring tone. "You know there isn't anything I wouldn't do for you. What's the problem?"

"It's not exactly a problem, Daddy," she said as she perched on the corner of his large oak desk. "I need to put a call through to Saudi Arabia—to accept a marriage proposal."

The senator couldn't hide his surprise. "Really, Christina—"

"Maybe I'd better explain," she said, amused by his response. She proceeded to explain, in great detail, the story of her courtship-by-mail and Joe's proposal, leaving out nothing. She had expected her father to be against her marrying Joe, but to her surprise, he wasn't at all opposed.

"If this is what makes you happy, darling," he told her.

"What about the call?" she wanted to know.

He gave a short laugh. "One thing about you, my dear—when you ask for something, you don't mess around, do you?" he asked.

"I wouldn't be your daughter if I did," she replied sweetly.

"Touché," he chuckled.

"Can you do it?"

He didn't hesitate. "I'll see what favors can be called in," he promised.

"I have good news for all of you—and even better news for me," Sergeant Lewis announced to his men. "You're all going home."

After a few moments of wild cheering from the men, Sergeant Lewis called them back to attention. "I'm not finished yet," he roared.

"That's one man I can look at and honestly predict—he'll never change," Dave whispered to Joe. "Even in the best of circumstances, he'll still be a jackass."

"So when do we leave?" someone in the crowd called out.

"You're not at ease yet," Lewis snapped in a menacing tone. "But you will be—day after tomorrow."

"That soon?" Joe was amazed.

"Friday morning, 0600 hours," the sergeant was saying.

Thirty-six hours, Joe thought. In thirty-six hours, I'll be going home.

He wished he knew what he'd be going home to.

"I can't believe it's so hard to get a call through to Saudi Arabia," Christina declared, annoyed. "I call Europe every day with no problem."

"Calling an office or a TV station or whatever in Paris is considerably different from calling a military installation in the Middle East, my dear," her father pointed out. "Getting through, depending on the current circumstances there, can be difficult—even impossible. I've done all I can to bypass the normal channels of communication."

"I know, Daddy, and I love you for it." She gave him a demonstrative hug. Looking at her father now, she saw not the powerful senator, the stern, unyielding public figure, or the silent, often remote man, but the warm, caring, doting father of her childhood. "I'm just anxious, that's all," she told him. "Anxious to give Joe my answer."

"Have you considered sending him a cable?" her father asked, trying to be as helpful as possible.

She nodded. "I suppose it's the only alternative," she conceded.

"I realize it's not as good as a phone call—" he started.

"No, it isn't," she agreed, shaking her head. She stood up, started for the door, then stopped and turned to face him again. "Have I told you I love you?" she asked.

He smiled. "You just did."

I give up, Joe thought, disgusted.

He'd gotten through to his mother, but not to Christina as of Thursday night. He'd been trying ever since he found out he was going home. With only hours left before he was to leave, he finally had to give up and resign himself to the fact that he wasn't going to be able to call her until he was back in the States.

I'll call her the minute we land at Andrews Air Force Base, he promised himself.

Heck, it'll be a local call from there. No problem.

Still, he wished he could go home knowing what her answer was going to be. Reluctantly, he returned to his tent to pack his gear.

Christina's cable, delayed by more of the same military red tape that had made a phone call impossible, arrived two hours after the plane he was on left Saudi Arabia.

Chapter Twelve

During the long, seemingly endless flight from Saudi Arabia to Washington, D.C., Joe found himself with a great deal of time on his hands and nothing to do but think—and think he did. A kaleidoscope of varied and conflicting images played in his mind like clips from a movie. Sometimes, those images featured Christina tearfully and joyfully accepting his marriage proposal; other times, he could see her regretfully telling him that she'd given it a great deal of thought and decided she couldn't possibly marry him, that the emotional and social gulf between them was simply too wide.

He wished he knew what he was going home to in terms of his future. And his son's.

He turned to Dave, who'd slept through most of the flight. Dave wasn't any better off—and he *knew* what he was going home to.

"What's the first thing you're going to do when you get home?" Joe asked, attempting conversation in a bid to take their minds off the boredom and the uncertainty.

"Shoot myself," Dave answered without hesitation.

"I'm serious."

"So am I." Dave paused. "Josie's going to marry that jerk."

Joe didn't know how to respond to that. "When did you find out?" he asked finally.

Dave frowned. "When I called home to let them know I was on my way. Apparently there was some kind of notice in the papers."

"I'm sorry," Joe said, and he meant it.

"Not half as sorry as I am. But thanks anyway, pal," said Dave sullenly.

Joe shook his head. Which was worse—knowing, or not knowing?

"What?" Christina couldn't believe what her father had just told her, so she asked him to repeat it.

"They've been called home," Winthrop Holland said. "They're on their way now."

The reality still hadn't fully sunk in. She didn't know whether to laugh or cry, a predicament she seemed to find herself in often these days. "Did he get my cable?" was her next question.

Her father shrugged. "We have no way of knowing at this point," he said truthfully.

Christina thought about it for a moment, trying to decide what to do next. "Can you find out what time—and where—he'll be arriving stateside?" she wanted to know.

He nodded, smiling. "Now *that* I can do," he said confidently. "Am I correct in assuming you want to be there when his plane lands?"

"If possible, yes."

"It'll only take a phone call," he promised.

Neither of them had seen her mother come into the study. Christina and her father exchanged a quick, questioning glance. "Don't you think you should tell her now?" The senator wanted to know.

"Tell me what?" Althea asked, realizing the moment she walked in on them that something important was going on.

Christina hesitated, but only for a moment. "Joe's asked me to marry him," she said almost apologetically. "I didn't tell you sooner, because I thought I should give Joe an answer."

"And have you?" Althea asked.

Christina shook her head. "I haven't been able to reach him—Daddy's been trying to help me get a call through, but now he's on his way home."

"And what will your answer be?" Althea asked, as if she hadn't already guessed.

"That, Mother, should be obvious," Christina said, knowing she was blushing.

Only a few more hours, Joe thought.

In just a few hours, they'd be landing at Andrews Air Force Base in Washington, D.C. He told himself he could call Christina from there as soon as they were on the ground. He could ask her again then.

Was he ready for her answer?

"Butterflies," Dave diagnosed, as if reading his mind.

"What?" Joe asked, not having heard him the first time.

"You have the worst case of butterflies I've ever seen," his friend told him.

"Is it that obvious?"

Dave chuckled, clearly enjoying his friend's predicament. "It couldn't be any more obvious if you had it tattooed on your forehead," he said.

Joe frowned. "If it's butterflies I've got in there," he said, patting his stomach, "they've got to be as big as the ones in those monster movies Max is so crazy about," he declared.

Well, Christina, what's it going to be? he wondered. Yes... or no?

"You won't have to go far to meet his plane," Christina's father informed her. "They're coming into Andrews."

"What time?" Christina wanted to know. Already the wheels were turning in her head, planning the perfect welcome for her fiancé.

Winthrop Holland looked at his watch. "In about two and a half hours."

Christina shrieked loudly. "That doesn't give me much time!"

Her father looked at her, puzzled. "Time? Time for what?"

"No time to explain now, Daddy—I'll tell you everything when I get back!" She was already halfway to the door.

"But, Christina—" he began.

"I love you, Daddy!" she called back to him as she ran out.

There was not a moment to waste. She'd finally come up with the perfect way to give Joe her answer.

Joe had it all figured out.

She didn't live far from the base. He knew that much. He'd take a taxi to her home and propose to her all over again—this time on bended knee, if necessary. On both knees, if that's what she wanted.

Whatever it takes, he vowed.

He loved her.

She'd told him she loved him, too.
He had to be optimistic.
It was that, or go crazy.

Irene Parrish called while Christina was getting dressed. "How wonderful to hear from you again so soon!" Christina told her sincerely, regretting even as she spoke that she'd have to cut their conversation short. "You do know Joe's coming home—"

"That's why I'm calling, dear. Joe has been trying to reach you—did he?"

"No—but my father found out he was coming home and when," Christina told her. "This call has to be costing you a great deal, all the way from Indiana—"

"We're not in Indiana, dear—that's why I'm calling," Irene said happily. "Max and I came down to meet Joe's plane. We thought you might like to go to the base with us."

"You're here?" As much as Christina adored Irene and Max, she was disappointed. She'd planned a romantic homecoming for Joe—and she had hoped to be alone when she met him at Andrews. But after a moment to think it over, she changed her mind. Under the circumstances, this was perfect.

"I'd love to, Irene," she told her future mother-in-law.

Where are the crowds? Joe wondered.

He'd expected some kind of turnout to welcome them home, even if on a smaller scale than the one that greeted the troops returning immediately after the war. But then, maybe that was just a tad unrealistic. The country was no longer at war, after all. They'd be lucky to have relatives waiting for them.

He doubted he'd have anyone there. His family lived too far away, and Christina didn't know he was coming.

"Well, this is it, pal." Dave's words cut through Joe's thoughts. "We're back on terra firma—at last."

"Feels like we've been in the air forever," Joe said wearily. Both men got to their feet and started collecting their things.

"At least we have one thing to be grateful for," Dave said with a forced optimism in his voice. "Where we come from, there isn't any *sand*."

"What the heck—!"

The shout had come from the front of the aircraft, near the open doors. A small group of men about to disembark from the plane were halted by something they'd seen outside. "What's going on?" Dave called out to them.

"You ain't gonna believe it—there's a woman out there on the tarmac!"

"All righhhhht!" someone else called out amid a chorus of catcalls.

"She's wearing a wedding dress!" another voice cried in disbelief.

"Yeah? Anybody here planning to get married within the next fifteen minutes?" someone wanted to know.

Dave's laugh was hollow. "Sucker!" was all he said.

Joe wasn't laughing. For a moment he wondered—no, it couldn't be. She didn't even know he was coming.

Or did she?

Her father was a U.S. senator.

His mother knew. And his mother might have told her.

Was it possible?

He started pushing his way through the crowd until he reached the front of the aircraft. "She ain't alone," someone announced as he made his way to the exit. "She's got another woman and a kid with her."

Another woman? A kid? Could his mother and Max be there? He squinted in the bright sunlight as he attempted a close look at the three people down on the tarmac. He saw Max right away...and there was his mother...and *Christina!*

"Hi, Dad!" Max called out, waving his arms wildly.

It *was* them—and Christina, in a white, cocktail-length dress and a bridal veil!

"Christina!" he cried out as he started down the ramp.

She waved. "Joe!"

He was in such a hurry to get to her that he almost fell down the ramp. She ran to meet him, with Max and Irene following closely behind. She was in tears when they collided in each other's arms.

"As long as you're already dressed for the occasion—will you marry me?" he asked, roaring with laughter at the spectacle she'd created.

She threw back her head and laughed. "I didn't think you'd even have to ask!"

Behind them, the crowd cheered wildly.

Epilogue

Five years later

The patio was decked out in multicolored balloons and streamers, and the long table where Christina's parents normally entertained during the summer or enjoyed alfresco breakfasts was draped with an equally colorful tablecloth—waterproof, of course. Children from two to twelve in casual attire and party hats lined either side of the table, armed with elaborately wrapped gifts. At the head of the table sat a little girl, today three years old, with curly blond hair and big blue eyes, dressed in a frilly white party dress and a pink foil party hat.

"She looks like she's having a good time," Joe commented as he and Christina, arms around each other's waists, observed the festivities from a respectable distance.

"Having a good time?" Christina laughed. "She's loving every minute of it!"

Joe gave her a playful squeeze. "She must get that from your mother."

Christina poked him. "And just what is *that* supposed to mean?" she asked.

"Ah, you know your mother. She'll use any excuse to throw a party," he reminded her.

"She's just a social creature," Christina sniffed with mock disdain.

"Social creature, my foot!" he chuckled. "If there were such a thing as Partyers Anonymous, Althea would be a charter member!"

Christina could laugh now. She could laugh and be happy. She and Joe had been married five years last month. Right after they'd settled into their new home here in Virginia— she'd been amazed he'd been willing to live anywhere outside Indiana!—and into their new life together, they'd decided to adopt a baby. And though the call from the adoption agency had taken its time coming, they'd finally been blessed with a baby.

A baby girl. Jennifer. The most beautiful baby Christina had ever seen. She could not have loved the infant more if she'd given birth to her herself.

Her little girl. Jennifer *was* her daughter now, just as Max was her son. She'd legally adopted Max at the same time she and Joe adopted Jennifer, and the day the adoptions became final was now a Parrish family holiday, one they celebrated every year as if it were a second Christmas, complete with gifts and a special dinner.

We'll eventually have that large family we both want, Christina thought confidently. We'll adopt a whole houseful of kids!

They'd already applied to adopt another child. Sex didn't matter, nor did the child's age. They hadn't asked for a baby, having a newborn didn't matter to Christina and Joe. They reasoned that there were a lot of older children out there in need of homes, and they were more than willing to provide one for as many as they could.

"Hey, Mom—Jennifer's spilled her ice cream!"

Max was at the center of that mob of children around the table. At fifteen, he was becoming a handsome—and responsible—young man, whose thoughts had already turned to what he wanted to do with his life. In just a few years, he'd be going off to study veterinary medicine in college, and Christina wasn't looking forward to the day he'd leave home. She already knew she was going to miss him terribly. She and Max had grown closer with each passing year, closer than some biological mothers and sons would ever be. Once again, she found herself wondering how Mindy Purcell could ever have turned her back on him.

If it hadn't hurt Joe and Max, I would count my blessings that she did, Christina told herself. Mindy's loss is my gain.

She looked up at Joe. Definitely my gain, she thought, certain that she had to be the luckiest woman in the world. Joe was a wonderful husband, tender and thoughtful and romantic. And he was a remarkable father, a pal and a confidant for Max as he grew older, and a doting daddy for Jennifer—though he'd insisted, quite strongly, that no one, under any circumstances, was to *ever* call her "Jenny."

"What are you thinking about?" Joe asked then, noticing the somewhat dreamy look on his wife's face.

She looked up at him. "You," she said simply, craning her neck to kiss him.

"Oh, well... in that case, the smile is perfectly understandable!" he chuckled, enjoying the knowledge that Christina had been thinking about him in the middle of all the festivities.

"Nut!" She poked his ribs again.

"Happy?" he wanted to know.

"Ecstatic," she assured him.

Their increasingly intimate conversation was interrupted by Christina's mother, who had emerged through the French doors. She called out to them in a tone that was unmistakably urgent. "Telephone," she informed them.

Joe twisted around, refusing to release his hold on Christina to do so. "Which one of us?" he wanted to know.

"Either of you—it's the adoption agency!" she told him.

Christina looked up at him anxiously. "I'll take it," he volunteered, giving her a reassuring kiss as he released her reluctantly and headed for the doors.

The next ten minutes seemed like ten hours for Christina—but when Joe returned, he was grinning from ear to ear.

"Well?" Christina demanded impatiently.

"We're about to become parents—again," he announced to all who cared to listen.

"A boy or a girl?" Christina wanted to know.

"A boy—and a girl." He took her in his arms. *"Twins!"*

* * * * *

Silhouette ROMANCE™

══ HEARTLAND ══ HOLIDAYS

Christmas bells turn into wedding bells for the Gallagher siblings in Stella Bagwell's *Heartland Holidays* trilogy.

THEIR FIRST THANKSGIVING (#903) in November
Olivia Westcott had once rejected Sam Gallagher's proposal—and in his stubborn pride, he'd refused to hear her reasons why. Now Olivia is back...and it is about time Sam Gallagher listened!

THE BEST CHRISTMAS EVER (#909) in December
Soldier Nick Gallagher had come home to be the best man at his brother's wedding—not to be a groom! But when he met single mother Allison Lee, he knew he'd found his bride.

NEW YEAR'S BABY (#915) in January
Kathleen Gallagher had given up on love and marriage until she came to the rescue of neighbor Ross Douglas...and the newborn baby he'd found on his doorstep!

Come celebrate the holidays with Silhouette Romance!

HEART

It's Opening Night in October—
and you're invited!
Take a look at romance with a
brand-new twist, as the stars
of tomorrow make their
debut today!
It's LOVE:
an age-old story—
now, with
*WORLD PREMIERE
APPEARANCES* by:

Patricia Thayer—Silhouette Romance #895
JUST MAGGIE—Meet the Texas rancher who wins this pretty teacher's heart...and lose your own heart, too!

Anne Marie Winston—Silhouette Desire #742
BEST KEPT SECRETS—Join old lovers reunited and see what secret wonders have been hiding...beneath the flames!

Sierra Rydell—Silhouette Special Edition #772
ON MIDDLE GROUND—Drift toward Twilight, Alaska, with this widowed mother and collide—heart first—into body heat enough to melt the frozen tundra!

Kate Carlton—Silhouette Intimate Moments #454
KIDNAPPED!—Dare to look on as a timid wallflower blossoms and falls in fearless love—with her gruff, mysterious kidnapper!

Don't miss the classics of tomorrow—
premiering today—only from

PREM

Take 4 bestselling love stories FREE

Plus get a FREE surprise gift!

Special Limited-time Offer

Mail to Silhouette Reader Service™

In the U.S.	In Canada
3010 Walden Avenue	P.O. Box 609
P.O. Box 1867	Fort Erie, Ontario
Buffalo, N.Y. 14269-1867	L2A 5X3

YES! Please send me 4 free Silhouette Romance™ novels and my free surprise gift. Then send me 6 brand-new novels every month, which I will receive months before they appear in bookstores. Bill me at the low price of $2.25* each—a savings of 44¢ apiece off the cover prices. There are no shipping, handling or other hidden costs. I understand that accepting the books and gift places me under no obligation ever to buy any books. I can always return a shipment and cancel at any time. Even if I never buy another book from Silhouette, the 4 free books and the surprise gift are mine to keep forever.

*Offer slightly different in Canada—$2.25 per book plus 69¢ per shipment for delivery. Canadian residents add applicable federal and provincial sales tax. Sales tax applicable in N.Y.

215 BPA ADL9   315 BPA ADMN

Name _____ (PLEASE PRINT) _____

Address _____ Apt. No. _____

City _____ State/Prov. _____ Zip/Postal Code _____

This offer is limited to one order per household and not valid to present Silhouette Romance™ subscribers. Terms and prices are subject to change.

SROM-92   © 1990 Harlequin Enterprises Limited

Silhouette ROMANCE™

★ WRITTEN IN THE STARS ★

WHEN A SCORPIO MAN MEETS A CANCER WOMAN

Luke Manning's broken heart was finally healed, and he vowed never to risk it again. So when this Scorpio man introduced himself to his neighbor, Emily Cornell, he had companionship on his mind—plain and simple. But just one look at the lovely single mom had Luke's pulse racing! Find out where friendship can lead in Kasey Michaels's PRENUPTIAL AGREEMENT, coming this November only from Silhouette Romance. It's WRITTEN IN THE STARS.

Available in November at your favorite retail outlet or order your copy now by sending your name, address, zip or postal code, along with a check or money order for $2.69 (please do not send cash), plus 75¢ postage and handling ($1.00 in Canada), payable to Silhouette Books to:

In the U.S.
3010 Walden Avenue
P.O. Box 1396
Buffalo, NY 14269-1396

In Canada
P.O. Box 609
Fort Erie, Ontario
L2A 5X3

Please specify book title with your order.
Canadian residents add applicable federal and provincial taxes.

SR1192